Producer & International Distributor
eBookPro Publishing
www.ebook-pro.com

RED VENGEANCE
Uzi Eilam

Translation: Jerry Hyman
Contact: eilamuzi@gmail.com

ISBN 9798397485999

Red

Vengeance

UZI EILAM

Contents

Chapter 1 - Moscow 7

Chapter 2 - Palo Alto.. 13

Chapter 3 - Tel Aviv and Berlin... 19

Chapter 4 - Tehran...27

Chapter 5 - Stanford 36

Chapter 6 - Arlington 41

Chapter 7 - Stanford 47

Chapter 8 - Tehran.. 57

Chapter 9 - Tel Aviv 68

Chapter 10 - Tehran 73

Chapter 11 - Pyongyang 79

Chapter 12 - Beirut and Tel Aviv 84

Chapter 13 - Beirut and Tel Aviv..92

Chapter 14 - Tehran 99

Chapter 15 - Palo Alto 105

Chapter 16 - Tel Aviv...112

Chapter 17 - Tehran and Moscow..117

Chapter 18 - Stanford 128

Chapter 19 - Tehran 135

Chapter 20 - Tel Aviv 149

Chapter 21 - Tehran 154

Chapter 22 - Tehran and Pyongyang 159

Chapter 23 - Tel Aviv 164

Chapter 24 - Moscow 174

Chapter 25 - Washington 178

Chapter 26 - Tel Aviv 190

Chapter 27 - Tehran 195

Chapter 28 - Tel Aviv 198

Chapter 29 - Tehran 203

Chapter 30 - Tel Aviv 208

Chapter 31 - Moscow 213

Chapter 32 - Stanford University 217

Chapter 33 - Tehran and Stanford 223

Chapter 34 - Stanford and Tehran 230

Chapter 35 - Stanford 234

Chapter 1

MOSCOW

President Vladimir Putin calls an emergency meeting to take place in the Politburo's conference room. Defense Minister Sergei Korchenko attends with his staff. Others in attendance include General Igor Kostkiukov, the head of military intelligence – the GRU – who arrives with the commander of the anti-aircraft forces, General Viktor Golubko, and the commander of the Air Force, Andrei Gomny. Defense Minister Korchenko is the only one who knows the purpose of the meeting, but he decides to wait for Putin to enter the room. The minister knows very well how to behave in order to ward off trouble. While they wait for Putin, the others exchange their opinions as to what is to be the subject of the meeting.

As the president enters they stand as one and salute.

Putin's words are spoken with outward calm, but the generals know there is a heavy hand behind the quiet demeanor. Silence in the room as Putin looks from one official to another. Judging by the attendees, it is obvious he will raise military and security issues. Those present try to guess the precise subject matter, and which of them will be the target of his disapproval.

"Sergei," Putin addresses the defense minister, "it is no secret that we have lost many soldiers from a direct attack. We suffered extensive impairment to the S-300 anti-aircraft battery and its operators. Can you provide a summary of the decisions in the last few days that most likely resulted in the severe damage to our anti-aircraft unit operating in northern Syria?"

"Of course, Honorable President," the minister is quick to reply, "We of course are all aware of our commitment to help Syria in the fight against traitors from within, terrorists who have occupied strategic sections of the country's territory. But we also must remember the aid we promised to defend Bashar al-Assad against threats from the outside, especially from Israel, whom we believe was responsible for this last attack—"

"So, the attack was the Israeli Air Force?" Putin cut in, "What do you know about this, Igor?" Putin demanded of the head of military intelligence, who did not dare to look up at him.

"We know with almost certainty that it was not an attack by the Americans—"

"Then who? The Syrian rebels, the Israelis, who?" Putin broke in, beginning to lose patience.

"This was an action by the Israelis," the Air Force commander spoke up, "even though we have an agreement with them that requires prior coordination for such action—"

"Agreement? We lost thirty fighters – soldiers and officers from our anti-aircraft personnel! Some of your best men, Viktor," Putin addressed the head of the anti-aircraft forces, "Why weren't they capable of defending themselves?"

"We received no prior warning of the attack, sir," the general tried to move the ball into the court of military intelligence. "In the initial investigation, our people thought these were Syrian planes, and—"

"And you didn't know, Igor? What happened to you?" Putin raised his voice at the head of military intelligence "Have you an explanation for this fiasco?"

"Commander..." stammered the head of intelligence. "There are too many factors stirring the pot here...and maybe several pots. The Syrian rebels who work against the government have already been mentioned, commander, and there is Turkish involvement on Syria's northern border. Hezbollah in Lebanon is also helping Bashar al-Assad in the war against the rebels. Iran supports Syria and Hezbollah and transfers weapons systems to the Lebanese organization, including precision missile technologies—"

"Do not bring up information here that is not new," Putin snapped at the head of intelligence, "What about information regarding the Israeli Air Force attack? Why wasn't that passed on to our anti-aircraft battery?"

"I am getting to that, sir, and I hope this will clarify matters. We track Israeli Air Force communications and know for certain that they are working to thwart the transfer of advanced weapons systems to Lebanon that come from Iran and pass through Syria. The Israelis are trying to stop Iran's continued involvement in Syria. The main factor in this arena is the Revolutionary Guard and especially the Quds Force, which acts as a sovereign state in itself. In the past, under General Soleimani we had more information, but now things are less clear. This is a new organizational setup."

"If I may," intervened the commander of the Air Force, "subsequent to what we have heard from the head of intelligence, Iranian aid to Hezbollah was carried out secretly by the Quds Force. They even concealed vital information from the Iranians themselves. On the other hand, we are certain that the Israelis have more information than we do concerning the moves of the Quds Force and they are constantly working to stop the arms transfers to Hezbollah. Our S-300 battery was targeted by them as aiding in the transfers that Iran sends through Syria. However, they should have informed us before entering Syrian airspace."

"Sir," chimed in the commander of anti-aircraft forces, "the battery and its men were to train Syrian crews to operate the S-300. They were not commissioned to take an active role. They did not activate the radar systems and therefore could not defend themselves. Our personnel have already visited the families who lost loved ones and are aiding them in every way possible."

"Any decision to cease operations is unacceptable. This is not to happen again. Damage to our battery has strategic and economic significance. We must maintain effectiveness and prevent loss of prestige with our customers. Take care of this," ruled Putin.

"It will be done, Commander," the general hastened to confirm.

"I would like to add, Honorable President," the commander of military intelligence spoke up, "and emphasize the overriding responsibility of the United States. Israel would not have dared to fly into Syria and damage Syrian and Iranian weapon systems and our elite unit as well, without the backing of the United States. The Americans must not be allowed to continue this support. It goes against everything we have invested so far in the region. I suggest we consider strategic punitive actions, more in the political sphere, as we did in the presidential election campaign of Donald Trump and Hillary Clinton. This will be much more effective than any tactical operation. But in addition, Mr. President, we must learn more about the derivative use of Artificial Intelligence, mainly in the field known as 'deepfake,' and the applications the Israelis use as well as new ones they are developing.

"Syria is vital to our foothold in the Middle East and our support for Assad must continue. As for Iran and Hezbollah, their aid suits us, but it is important to maintain a strategic balance when it comes to the positions of Israel and the United States. I therefore direct our air force to maintain contacts to coordinate with the Israeli Air Force. And from you, General Kostkiukov, I expect a plan that I will call 'strategic political punishment' to prevent the Americans and the Israelis from interfering in Syria. Above all, we must make them stop supporting the rebels against the Assad regime." commanded Putin.

"We have other assets, drones of all sizes, but mostly highly accurate ultrasonic missiles in our arsenal," said the defense minister.

"This is the flagship of our advanced technology. I approved making it available to Iran. What is the state of their control of this technology?"

"They are making progress. We have made clear to the Iranians their obligation to maintain the highest level of security on this issue. The leader of the project is the Iranian scientist Doctor Madani, who leads a small team of experts within the framework of the Quds Force..."

"I haven't heard yet when the project is due to be completed! What is the 'highest level of security?' Do you have a good answer, Igor?" Putin turned to the head of military intelligence.

"We instructed Doctor Madani to keep the subject strictly confidential...this means there is a slow rate of adoption of the technology."

"These supersonic missiles have an intercontinental range and are immune to detection by the current systems being used," the Minister of Defense intervened, "there is logic to the security limitations. We have learned the hard way that Iran is sometimes vulnerable to American and Israeli intelligence."

"I have categorically decided on the transfer of the supersonic technology of the missiles. This is not a topic for discussion," Putin furiously banged on the table. "You have a lot of work to do, gentlemen, and not a moment to waste. Get to it!" he ordered, as he rose from his chair and left the room.

Chapter 2

PALO ALTO

Noam returned home from university after a full day in the research laboratory and waited somewhat anxiously for Dan. He was late as usual. She had already looked over the file with the latest updates of deepfake technologies several times. It featured a bizarre dialogue between former President Barack Obama and the Iranian Foreign Minister in which Obama spoke exactly like Trump, arguing against the nuclear agreement that he himself had promoted. The Iranian foreign minister sounded gratified and paid the former president lavish compliments. A rushed NSA report of this strange exchange was shown only to a limited circle that Dan and Noam were privileged to belong to. The report determined that the entire dialogue was deep and totally fake, noting the peculiarities, and concluded by saying they were working on uncovering the source. Noam read over the material three more times, making notes of the points she would raise with Dan.

The rattle of the key was heard and the front door swung open.

"Hi, Dandush. Finally! I was starting to worry," Noam exclaimed and hugged her husband, who poured them both their end-of-the-day drinks; bourbon for him, chardonnay for her.

"Did something special happen? Anything new?"

Noam showed Dan the report and the points she wanted to raise.

"We should talk to Deutsch and arrange a meeting with him at SRI in the morning. I'm sure he's in the picture with his good relationship with the agencies. I assume the Russians are involved in this."

"And what was today like at work?"

"I am happy to say, my dear that 'New Future' is in pretty good shape. The company's been doing great even while I was away. After a long struggle in Washington, we finally signed a serious contract with the Pentagon for the development of advanced systems for combating terrorist organizations. We got a lot of credit thanks to the campaign we'd waged against Iranian terrorism."

"That's terrific! Is that why we got this file?"

Dan smiled, picked up his glass of bourbon, and took a pleasurable sip. Noam joined with her Californian Chardonnay, and for a moment, the two of them quietly enjoyed their drinks. Noam looked into Dan's eyes.

"Is there anything else you wanted to update me on?" she asked.

"Gideon called today and we know he doesn't call the company without good reason. He wanted to congratulate us on the Pentagon project and I filled him in on it."

"And what else did my father want?"

"He sent regards from Nahari, the head of the Mossad..."

"Just like that, out of nowhere?"

"I understood that Nahari informed your father of what Evyatar and his men discovered about a big move brewing in the Russia-Iran-North Korea triangle."

"What do we have to do with it? Now that we have finally started to lead a quiet life with interesting technological challenges, Nahari can find himself new recruits for his wars and let both my father and us have a little peace."

"The Iranian supreme leader is not satisfied that revenge for the murder of Soleimani hasn't been carried out. He's demanding action from the Quds Force. Russia was mentioned when the Iranians began planning payback for the attempts to get at the scientist leading their nuclear research. Nahari and Gideon just want to keep us in the loop."

"We'll see what develops. Meantime I have questions on the latest technologies and of course about deepfake that we can discuss with Deutsch at the institute tomorrow. I think it has to do with the face recognition issues I am working on."

Noam opened her laptop and began typing at the phenomenal speed that always surprised Dan.

"What exactly do you want to focus on?" asked Dan.

"I recently learned about the progress in Artificial Intelligence and found the derivative of 'deepfake' there. This could tie in well with the face recognition theme from my thesis. I know you can help me get through the temporary information barrier."

"Deepfake is an AI-based technology used to create fake photos, videos, or sound clips. The term was coined by combining 'deep learning' and 'fake.' Deepfake's capabilities enable it to publish false news, media spins to manipulate public opinion that in many cases will influence election results."

"At this point, I'm more interested in the academic aspect, Dan. I saw that the basis of academic research is mainly in the field of computer vision. How does that relate to facial expressions?"

"The software development began a few years ago at the academy. It takes existing video clips of a person speaking and synchronizes his speech with a different vocal track. This is done through 'machine learning' that creates a connection between the voice produced by the person in the video and the shape of his face. One of the senior scientists in our company will put together a review of important articles of interest for you."

"In general, what are the applications of the technology in the civilian sphere? Mainly politics?"

"Yes. There are defensive and offensive applications that have already received coverage in the media, but most of the parties that operate in these areas keep the information to themselves. We saw the uproar caused by 'Cambridge Analytica' not long ago. The investigation into its involvement in the election process that led to the victory of Donald Trump in the United States is a prime example. The company manipulated public opinion in dozens of other countries, including Great Britain, during the fight over Brexit. Cambridge Analytica's illegal use of materials it had gathered from

Facebook led to an investigation that ultimately caused it to close down operations. Another example is the use of deepfake audio for massive transfers of funds. It's common knowledge that the CEO of a British energy company received and carried out telephonic instructions from the CEO of the parent company to transfer 220,000 Pounds Sterling to a bank in Hungary. Another example was the broadcast of a video clip taken from a speech by Nancy Pelosi, the Democratic Speaker of the House. The production included slowing down her rate of speaking and changing the pitch so that she sounded drunk. Many listeners claimed it wasn't fake. Another strictly civilian use of deepfake is to promote the sales of fashion products. This use of the technology allows a view of the whole body."

"So how do we develop a means to identify deepfake and other fakes? How can we compete and defend against the murderous rate of Artificial Intelligence development? And how does this contribute to the formation of defense systems against the malicious use of deepfake in fake news and other uses?"

"Making fake news capabilities available to the general public is not necessarily a bad thing. Of course, there is the danger that the tools will reach more bad actors, but these threats operate under the auspices of the state and they can be controlled. We expect to see a major increase in deepfake videos that everyone knows are phony, and that's a positive thing overall."

"Isn't that a contradiction? How can an increase in bad actors be a good thing?"

"It seems like a contradiction, but when you look

deeper, you come to an interesting conclusion: the more people are exposed to deepfake videos distributed in large quantities, the more they will begin to recognize fake information with its small glitches and 'screw-ups' that will help Artificial Intelligence systems to identify them. You could compare it to the use of vaccines in the healthcare field where a person is injected with an inert or weakened virus, which stimulates the body's defense system to produce healthy antibodies.

"The next step for me will be to integrate deepfake technology into the algorithms I developed for facial recognition," Noam declared. She stood up and went to Dan, giving him an especially warm hug.

"That's enough for now. Let's gather strength for another day of new discoveries."

"Well," answered Dan, and said with a smile, "that's an offer I can't refuse, my dear."

Chapter 3

TEL AVIV AND BERLIN

Dr. Gideon Ben Ari enjoys the quiet of managing the technology consulting company he founded. Scientific challenges continue to fascinate him. He was satisfied that he had fulfilled his mission in a tumultuous period, leading the fight against Iranian terrorism from within the Israeli Mossad – where he felt "at home." Thus, the huge pile of documents on his desk and the vast number of emails he received did not bother him at all. And Noga, his faithful secretary, always made sure to spoil him with a cup of aromatic coffee and a generous slice of delicious crumb cake.

Gideon was well aware that his extensive operational experience in the war against Iranian terrorism had enhanced his reputation as a consultant for companies in Israel and abroad. He had gained valuable expertise as commander of a paratroop unit in retaliatory operations. In the ensuing years, he'd accrued a large quantity of material that enabled him to offer advisory services in the fields of cyber warfare and defense against advanced technological threats.

The ringing of the internal telephone suddenly broke the silence. Noga informed Gideon that Nahari, the head of the Mossad, wanted a meeting for the purpose of updating him.

Gideon grumbled to Noga. "Nahari has apparently forgotten that I retired from dealing with Iranian terrorism. They even gave me a farewell party in the office with the heroic team I led. He also probably forgot my recommendation to put his trust in the kids: Dan, Noam, Evyatar, and Eric. They're already grown-ups... But I can't refuse Nahari. Oh, Noga, I need you to compile the material I need for the science conference I'm invited to at the Free University of Berlin. I was going to tell Nahari about it anyway."

Gideon loved the peace and quiet that was now his lot and was happy to receive invitations to international conferences concerning Artificial Intelligence and advanced technologies. However, it was clear that an appeal from Nahari would come at some point.

***

"Good morning, Gideon!" Nahari exclaimed with unusual enthusiasm when Gideon entered. "Thank you for coming in so quickly. We haven't actually seen each other in a long time, with you being busy with technological consulting, far from all the difficulties of dealing with the war on terror."

"You know I would not ignore your call to the flag even after we agreed to pass the baton on to the younger generation," said Gideon. "Nevertheless, I emphasize again, Nahari, that trust should be given to the young people: Dan, Noam, Evyatar, and the relatively new addition, Dr. Eric Grossfeld."

The two exchanged knowing glances. Eric Grossfeld was the alias provided for Nimer's son Hassan, to keep him safe.

"Yes, yes, Gideon, I remember you recommended considering both you and Nimer as senior advisors. I didn't forget that. And speaking of Nimer, how is he doing in Berlin at the Free University?"

"I'm in secretive contact with Nimer. I don't want to endanger him and reveal the connection. The Iranians and Hezbollah are still trying to find him wherever he is and eliminate him. In the meantime, he has succeeded in securing a respectable academic position for himself. He's leading extensive research on Artificial Intelligence and its derivatives. That reminds me to update you about the invitation I received to a civilian academic conference there," Gideon hastened to reassure Nahari when he noticed his inquisitive look. "They invited me to join a round table on the applications of these technologies in the expanding civilian market. The whole conference will be about innovations in smart algorithms for Artificial Intelligence, machine learning, data mining systems and the recent headlines that deepfake has been making."

"Will you be the only Israeli there?"

"No. Scientists from Rafael, engineers from Israel Aerospace Industries, and researchers from Elbit are participating. Everyone knows Israel has something to contribute to these fields and the Germans appreciate that fact. The conference opens in two days from now and I plan to fly to Berlin tomorrow. I had a meeting with the young people and learned some things I didn't know. I was extremely impressed by Eric's knowledge and what Noam contributed," Gideon answered the unasked question.

"Very good, Gideon, it sounds like a good opportunity to catch up on what's happening. As far as Nimer is concerned, you know best how to handle the meetings with him. Have a good trip!"

***

El Al's business class lounge was packed as usual with passengers who kept working on their laptops, promoting their technological and business issues. Gideon got himself an espresso and found a seat at an empty table. He surveyed the hall and was soon joined by two other passengers, a Rafael representative and a man from Israel Aerospace Industries, who hastened to introduce themselves. Gideon was pleased that despite the considerable amount of time that had passed since he was a central figure in security matters, people still remembered him. He enjoyed the conversation with the two younger men until they announced boarding for the flight.

Artificial Intelligence, advanced algorithms, machine learning, data mining, and the advent of deepfake were no longer foreign to Gideon's ears. He found the organization of the conference to be excellent. It began with a reception at the airport where many of the conference participants had arrived. Everyone benefited from the dedicated and devoted care of the conference organizers. They provided transportation and booked accommodation at "Adlon Kempinski," an excellent hotel in the heart of Berlin.

A fancy thick tote bag was waiting at the reception desk for each of the participants. Gideon was not surprised by the elegant suite made available to him. He sat in the plush armchair and opened the folder with the conference schedule and background data, and was surprised to see a handwritten note fall from it to the floor. There was no signature but it was not hard for Gideon to distinguish who wrote it – Nimer, who congratulated him on attending the conference and added only, "See you at dinner tonight." It's good that Nimer was keeping in contact, thought Gideon, looking over the note again. We need to find an opportunity to talk and this only strengthens me in that resolve, Gideon concluded, before tearing the note into little pieces.

Gideon's laptop contained the details about Artificial Intelligence he'd gathered in his update with Evyatar, Dan, and Noam.

***

"Hello, Dr. Ben Ari! Thank you for agreeing to participate in this important conference," Gideon heard the familiar voice. He looked up and smiled, raising his glass of champagne to his childhood friend who responded to Gideon's "Cheers" with his glass of orange juice. "Hello to you too, Doctor Grossfeld. Good to see you," replied Gideon. "I take it you're on the conference organizing committee. It looks great, very promising," Gideon complimented him.

"Thank you, Dr. Ben Ari. Really, we, that is, all the conference attendees are impressive. May I call you Gideon?"

"Certainly, Dieter, with pleasure," Gideon hastened to answer. "I'm sure you're busy and I won't take up your time. We'll find time to talk tomorrow or the day after."

"That's fine, Gideon. Have a nice evening and see you later at the conference sessions," Nimer promised.

***

The Kempinski Hotel fitness center had all the most advanced equipment and Gideon did not forego his usual morning workout. Only one other person was there, on the exercise bike. Gideon was surprised to see it was Nimer himself.

"Good morning, Dieter," Gideon called out. "I see that you too are addicted to morning exercise."

"Yes, Gideon. Just so you know I had someone to learn from and I find time for a half hour every morning. It's a great start to the day."

"That's exactly how I feel. It's another common interest for us besides Artificial Intelligence and advanced technology. Have a good day. See you later," Gideon said, as he went for a walk on the treadmill.

***

The first day's sessions were full of innovations. Gideon contributed extensively to the topics discussed at the round table on civilian uses of Artificial Intelligence derivatives. The lectures ended with a festive dinner for all the participants. Gideon was pleased to find himself seated next to Doctor Dieter Grossfeld at the lecturers' table. The general atmosphere was relaxed and it was obvious that the speakers who had already participated in the discussions were breathing a sigh of relief. Gideon managed to slip into the conversations, an invitation to Nimer to end the evening with a cup of coffee in Gideon's suite. The meal now seemed to him to be long enough and he was impatient for it to end.

"We've had a long day," Gideon addressed his neighbors at the table, "and tomorrow another long day awaits." He said goodnight and headed for the elevator.

It wasn't long before there was a knock on the door. Nimer entered the suite and the two childhood friends hugged each other.

"You don't have a problem with our special relationship being revealed?" Gideon asked worriedly. "No, Gideon, I am on the management team for the conference and our meeting seems natural and part of the organizing activity. There have been lots of advances and we have little time, so let's talk about what's been happening in the areas that occupied us in the past."

For a good hour, the two friends filled each other in on what had transpired recently. Nimer spoke of how good he felt on the staff of the University in Berlin. He proudly updated Gideon on the academic success of his son - who was now called Eric Grossfeld. Gideon had his own proud description of his daughter Doctor Noam Avni and her husband Dan. Nimer said that Eric was going to do post-doctorate work at the SRI Institute at Stanford. Both Nimer and Gideon made sure not to touch on security issues and Gideon only talked about his agreement with Nahari on passing the baton to the young people. He also clarified that both of them would remain strategic advisors to the Mossad and especially to Nahari himself.

"So how do you think we can maintain this position?" asked Nimer. "We need to find a safe way to keep up to date to be 'worthy' of the title of strategic advisers to Nahari."

"We can think about continuing some of the studies that are being presented at the conference and keep up an Israel-German connection that would justify mutual visits."

"For greater security, I will endeavor to become a member of the university's tenured staff but not a leader. I also welcome the relationship the Avni family has with my son and I would be incredibly happy to meet with him in conjunction with our joint scientific activity." Nimer said.

"Absolutely. Yes, my friend, this is the direction we should take," Gideon responded, as he stood up to part from Nimer.

Chapter 4

TEHRAN

The supreme leader of Iran convened an extraordinary meeting.

The entire top echelon of the national leadership was called in for it: The president of the Republic, the foreign minister, the commander of the Revolutionary Guards, the head of the Ministry of Intelligence and National Security, and the commander who had just been appointed to lead the Quds Force, General Kashani. They all gathered in the leader's modest discussion room, whispering among themselves, trying to fathom the purpose of the meeting. The presence of a scientist who came in with General Kashani was also the subject of curious whispers. "What has the researcher Doctor Madani from the Quds Force have to do with these proceedings and discussion with the leader?" Wondered the commander of the Revolutionary Guards in a thunderous half-whisper.

"Please be seated, gentlemen. I thank you for coming," the leader addressed them as he entered the room and sat at the head of the long conference table. "There are important matters to discuss, quite complex..."

No one spoke, waiting intently for the leader's next words.

"We have lost General Soleimani, may Allah avenge his blood, murdered by despicable assassins. Do you, in the Ministry of Intelligence and National Security, have any clues that can lead us to the killers?" demanded the leader, suddenly raising his voice, which was unusual for him. "It is essential we know exactly how it happened so we may be better protected in the future. We must be certain of the identity of the assassins in order to eradicate them. That is all we are waiting for."

"Indeed, the recent loss of the martyred General Soleimani, commander of the Quds Force was almost certainly carried out by the Americans. However, your decree calling for revenge has not yet been received," General Kashani dared say.

"Had we received information in time about the plot from our intelligence agency, we could have prevented it, and the commanding general of the illustrious Quds Force would still be with us," added the Revolutionary Guards commander in sharp criticism of the intelligence division and the Quds Force.

"And we have not forgotten the damage to the uranium enrichment program," the foreign minister broke in. "Even today we do not have the means to block the cyber Stuxnet worm that was used on the Natanz nuclear site. And just recently, our enemies also managed to severely damage the facilities in Natanz with a huge blast they were able to trigger on the centrifuge site deep within the earth. We have seen concrete-penetrating bombs used here before. Only the Americans who developed them have the capacity for an attack with such a powerful explosive charge. Unfortunately, we learned of their intention to bomb Natanz only after it occurred."

May I suggest, Honorable Leader, that the head of intelligence be allowed to continue his important review," the president of the Republic interceded, mainly to stop the intrusion of the commander of the Revolutionary Guards. The wars between the top generals had been raging for a long while. The discussion clearly revealed in all its strength the struggle for succession, encouraged by the failing health of the supreme leader "The president is right. Please continue," the leader urged the head of the Ministry of Intelligence.

"Let us not forget that the professor of nuclear science was and remains a target for a host of enemy security services. We have tracked down and foiled five attempted operations to compromise the professor as well as a few others of our best people. We concentrated our efforts mainly against the Israeli Mossad and the American CIA. Today we know almost with complete certainty that an elite operations unit of the Israeli Mossad attempted unsuccessfully to assassinate the scientist."

"We seek justice, Your Holiness, in countering a potential operation against the director of the nuclear project," insisted the commander of the Revolutionary Guards. "Perhaps we will hear from the new commander of the Quds Force what is causing the delay in taking revenge despite you, our leader, having made it top priority?" General Kashani posed the question to the supreme leader.

The floor is yours, General Kashani," encouraged the leader.

"I think, Your Holiness, that all of us were informed of the initiative of General Soleimanpour, the commander of the Quds Force in Argentina. We were all aware of his plan to attack the embassies of the United States and Israel in Buenos Aires. We supported this initiative and the general had a free hand to plan and carry out the missions. But this was not the only Quds Force initiative he put forth in South America. Without our knowledge, Soleimanpour made an agreement with a Nazi organization in South America called 'Odessa,' and planned a brazen and highly sensitive attack on the Catholic Pope. The supreme leader ordered us to investigate the conduct of the Quds Force headquarters in Argentina, and we have withheld approval of the scheme. Doctor Madani, who we will now hear from, will present his findings from a trip he made to Buenos Aires."

"What news can the young doctor bring to us?" The commander of the Revolutionary Guards grumbled. "We have already heard about the unholy association of Soleimanpour with 'Odessa,' and the ruling out of assassinating the Pope, as well as the subsequent trial that dealt with this flagrant abuse of authority. It is well known that he was found guilty and is serving a prison sentence for..."

"We will hear from Doctor Madani," the leader interceded, and did not permit the commander of the Revolutionary Guards to continue.

Now it all hangs on my report, thought Madani to himself as he opened his laptop with shaking hands. *"How do I convey to this cabal of generals, who are generally not supportive, information concerning political and technological complications that I was exposed to in the meeting with Soleimanpour in Argentina?"*

Madani gathered his thoughts and continued.

"The plans for revenge for the murder of General Soleimani seemed appropriate to us and we were confident of their implementation in a far-off geographical location in Buenos Aires. On the face of it, it seemed to me a proper use of advanced technologies with attack drones and precision missiles. There was also backup for the attack on the embassies with vehicles containing car bombs. These would be activated by young Lebanese fighters trained by instructors from Hezbollah. They were to operate autonomously in the final stage of the attack if the previous measures were to fail..."

"All this intricate planning did not work efficiently!" The commander of the Revolutionary Guards burst out. "We paid a heavy price for our people who were killed."

"I am getting to that, Honorable Commander of the Guards, and I will not skip over the affair of the assassination plot of the Pope in the Vatican. I promise to present my conclusions and the lessons learned," Madani replied, feeling more confident, thanks to the supreme leader's support. "The plan for the attacks devised by the commander of the Quds Force in Argentina was a good one, but it did not take into account the disparity of the technological forces. The young Lebanese were enthusiastic, but not well enough trained. The other measures also were technologically inferior to what the Americans and the Israelis had at their disposal."

"Doctor Madani," queried the foreign minister, "perhaps you can clarify this story of the Nazi organization, Odessa? What motivated General Soleimanpour to collaborate with them? Especially on such a delicate issue as an attempted assassination of the Pope?"

"This issue, Honorable Minister of Foreign Affairs," intervened General Kashani, "was discussed at length at the trial. We have heard about the financial contributions of the Nazis to the activities of Moscow that disrupt the Quds Force in South America. This particularly concerns the assassination attempt against Pope Francis, which fortunately did not go forward." The supreme leader signaled to the foreign minister to cease speaking and encouraged Madani with a look and a wave of his hand to continue.

I must add," Madani continued with confidence, "that my investigation in Buenos Aires revealed an arrogant pompousness on the part of the general. He claimed that we in Tehran do not understand the facts on the ground in South America. This is an opinion that in the past, in light of the general's successes, may have been justified, but not any longer. The lessons we learned are focused both on the unfortunate choice of operational fighters and the lack of consideration of technological inferiority that enabled the enemy to block our plans."

"Your Holiness," insisted the commander of the Revolutionary Guards, "the questions concerning our response to the murder of General Soleimani and the serious damage to the uranium enrichment plant at Natanz remain unanswered..."

"Doctor Madani has not concluded his review," General Kashani, commander of the Quds Force, came to the aid of the scientist, encouraged by the leader's affirmative nod. Madani went on.

"Indeed, the recent operations by the Israeli Mossad, probably also with the help of traitors at home, were focused on nuclear issues. But we will not give up taking revenge on the murderers of General Soleimani. It is important to continue his legacy to aid the countries and organizations that help us spread Shiism, especially Syria and Hezbollah in Lebanon. Also, assistance from North Korea in Artificial Intelligence and cyberwarfare is indispensable for any revenge attack," Madani confidently concluded.

"Doctor Madani is right in stressing the importance of spreading the Shia in the world and especially in the Middle East that Soleimani had been carrying out with such impressive success," intervened the foreign minister. "Russia has shown that it has an interest in this direction as well as a strategic, tactical, and technological ability to continue its aid in Syria. I would like to emphasize the fact that the Russians supported us in the completion of the nuclear power reactor in the city of Bushehr. This was after the Germans gave in to American pressure and canceled their work on the construction of the reactor. The Russians stood by us also during our negotiations with the six powers on the nuclear agreement. Our response, Honorable Leader, to the attempted murder of the director of our nuclear program and the damage to the Natanz enrich-ment plant must be the swift continuation of progress on the nuclear development project."

"I will summarize and present the challenges that must be faced," the supreme leader raised his voice. "We need to upgrade our capabilities in the cyber field and encourage our friends from North Korea to help us even more than in the past. For the murder of General Soleimani, the United States should be punished and this time in a new, more severe manner without our having to put trust in fighters from Hezbollah. As for our reaction to the assassination attempts on the pro-fessor of nuclear sciences, I recommend approving the words of the Minister of Foreign Affairs - acting vigor-ously to continue the development of nuclear weapons. We will be aided by the decision of the American Pres-ident Trump who canceled the United States' partici-pation in the nuclear agreement. I ask that you think about our capability in the field of long-range mis-siles and ways to use this capability in addition to all that was mentioned. A final critical point concerns the strengthening of the relationship with Russia, mainly in support of Syria, and also in the ways in which Mos-cow aspires to have an influence in the Middle East in general. We are not concerned only with political sup-port, but also aid in advanced technology such as cyber, Artificial Intelligence, deepfake, and more."

"I support every word Doctor Madani has presented, Honorable Leader, and I will assign the best of Quds Force personnel to carry out the missions," Kashani promised.

No one else of those gathered in the room spoke up and the supreme leader concluded: "I approve the main recommendations of Dr. Madani, which are supported by General Kashani, commander of the Quds Force. Gentlemen, you have one week to present complete plans for approval to deal with what we have heard here today. The Commander of the Quds Force and Doctor Madani will head these operations. Thank you all."

Chapter 5

STANFORD

Gerald Deutsch, Ph.D. in Physics and Systems analysis, fought as an officer in Vietnam and later served in a senior position at the Pentagon. The forward-thinking Deutsch was recruited by the intelligence services and various federal agencies thanks to his comprehensive vision and excellent relationships with associates. Over the years he had kept up a long-standing association with Gideon Ben Ari. Deutsch's involvement in preventing Iranian terrorist activity in California was the reason he was asked once again to assist the Mossad. It was good to return to the institute; it meant a change from the mad pace of battling Iranian terrorism, Deutsch thought as he sat in his office at the institute and planned his agenda for the day. There was plenty to do without having to deal every minute with only the security applications of technology. In a few minutes, the brainstorming session with senior researchers he had scheduled would begin. Its objective was to determine the institute's role in implementing new, advanced technologies.

"Good morning, gentlemen. Today we are going to focus on new applications for Artificial Intelligence. I trust you've read the background material I sent you on new developments. Our aim is to examine what we can learn about adopting its capabilities. The arms race and technological competition between the superpowers has been going on for years. Military usage of AI has been extremely important for these nations. They benefitted from a significant edge in the early years from their security agencies. But today, it appears that civilian applications of AI take precedence."

"The material you passed on to us," ventured the associate for Future Studies, "is impressive, and I would say a somewhat confusing assortment of technologies that grew out of the scientific infrastructure for Artificial Intelligence. For example, face recognition, deepfake audio and video, fake news, and also recently developed systems for detecting the prevalent use of fakes. These are mainly security and political issues, Doctor Deutsch. Where does civilian application come into the picture?"

"It's true, the first push for AI applications was in the security and political fields. My experience in the war on Iranian terror is an example. The achievement of Dr. Noam Avni in the successful application of face recognition helped in the fight against terrorism and especially in derailing the plot to assassinate the Pope. However, I believe it is vital that we now take SRI in a new direction towards civilian usage, and establish ourselves as a leader in these technologies..." The enthusiastic nodding of heads to this last statement showed that Deutsch knew very well how to motivate and arouse enthusiasm in his colleagues.

"Correct me if I'm wrong," the associate continued. "I think the importance of Artificial Intelligence for civilian use is that it increases support for the economy, enables the development of new medications, contributes to the efficiency and safety of transportation, and allows for a keener understanding of the global climate."

"Precisely," Deutsch responded, "and you can add the six main subsets of Artificial Intelligence: machine learning, deep learning, robotics, neural networks, natural language processing, genetic algorithms, as well as the Internet of Things, which is already an important element in our military and civilian toolbox. Basically, it is all about developing digital capabilities for connecting to communication networks and being able to transmit and receive everything that appears on the networks."

"Something is not clear to me, Doctor Deutsch," the associate broke in. "The agreements we signed with the Pentagon, which provides a significant portion of our budget, are only for security issues. We have existing contracts on these intelligence issues. We've developed algorithms for autonomous weapon systems and autonomous vehicles. We have additional contracts with the Pentagon to develop command and control systems to handle massive data. Is it your intention to abandon the entire security field in favor of concentrating solely on civilian usage of AI?"

"I don't intend to leave the security field entirely, but rather to use the foothold we have in it, and leverage it to become a leader in civilian usage as well. There is a close connection between defense activity and the advancement of technologies in the civilian field, which has benefited greatly from the technological groundwork developed in security and defense..."

Deutsch stopped speaking when his secretary came in and announced he had an urgent call from the Pentagon. The Assistant Secretary of Defense, retired Lt. Gen. Thomas Dayton, was on the line. Deutsch entrusted the running of the meeting to the research associate and left for his office.

"Hello, Deutsch," began the general, "thanks for making yourself available for my call. We recently set up another special think tank and I want you to join us."

"Thomas, my friend," replied Deutsch, "I couldn't refuse to participate in a task that I have no doubt is important, even without knowing the details. In short, what's on the agenda this time?"

"Well, briefly, and confidentially, let's say we are analyzing a sensitive and threatening strategic development of Russia's involvement in the Middle East that has to do with the Iranian connection. Let me add that the defense secretary and the newly elected president himself are in the picture, urging us to come up with ways to deal with this new threat. I'll fill you in when we meet."

Deutsch was not surprised to find a US Air Force executive jet warming up its engines when he arrived at San Francisco International Airport. But he hadn't been expecting such a warm welcome from the commander of the security team appointed to accompany him. The officer greeted Deutsch with the special salute of the Navy Seals and proudly stated his team was made up of "Seal Team 6" fighters, the most famous of the Seals.

Deutsch gingerly climbed up the steps to the plane, which took off immediately...

Chapter 6

ARLINGTON

Entering the subterranean level in the Pentagon took Deutsch back to the time when he was stationed there. He was pleased to meet the assistant secretary of defense and two veteran research officers who were members of the think tank after the September 11 attacks. Deutsch and General Dayton shook hands warmly, the latter hastening to say that Deutsch would continue to serve as the liaison with the Israelis and that the briefing was for him to share information with the others.

Deutsch followed the assistant secretary through the corridors of the subterranean floor and could not shake the feeling of surprise about a spy cell that purportedly works for Israel without being sure if it even existed. The three research officers and the NSA man rose as one as the assistant secretary and Deutsch entered the special conference room. They introduced themselves briefly at the request of the assistant secretary. Deutsch was impressed by the diversity of fields of knowledge of those present, and their obvious technological and intelligence expertise. All three from the Pentagon and the senior officer from the NSA were in combat in Afghanistan and had impressive scientific careers with doctorates from leading universities in the United States. They had published papers on cyber technology and had comprehensive knowledge of Artificial Intelligence.

"Thomas, I think it's for you to tell me specifically what you expect me to accomplish here, don't you?" asked Deutsch after the brief introductions. He felt comfortable with his friend from the past and made clear he had every intention of being of help.

"I think you'll find it worth hearing what the NSA knows about a deepfake which Russia has just perpetrated."

The assistant secretary nodded to the senior research officers to begin.

"The alarm bells went off when Russia changed course on everything regarding the assistance it decided to provide Iran on their nuclear program..."

"And what motivated Russia to make such a dangerous move?" the assistant secretary interrupted, "It seems to me that Putin is taking considerable risks here."

"That's true, and unfortunately, we do not have complete information on what motivated Putin," the officer apologized. "Part of the answer to your question lies in the area that Doctor Deutsch also remembers from the time when he was a member of our strategic research team here. I'm referring to President Reagan's strategic defense initiative - 'Star Wars'...

"I remember that very well. The confrontation of the

strategic team I was part of, with the critics and opponents of the proposal, and also from technological circles, to what they called 'Reagan's Star Wars dream,'" Deutsch shared from his past experience. "The most prominent supporter was Edward Teller, the father of the hydrogen bomb. He backed the idea unequivocally, the ability to develop and equip defense systems in space," Deutsch continued and said with a certain nostalgia, "but the project didn't get to the finish line and only projects like the anti-missile missile 'Arrow' developed in Israel with American support and THAAD, the American Terminal High Altitude Area Defense missile against long-range ballistic missiles. These developments relied on the technological infrastructure garnered by the space defense initiative. But...what connection does that have to do with Russia's moves today?"

"The American program," the officer replied, "included laser systems carried by satellites to intercept missiles from space, supercomputers to calculate ballistic trajectories, X-ray-based systems, and similar technologies. The Soviet Union at that time was deeply entrenched in Afghanistan, draining blood, and spending money in quantities it couldn't afford. A huge strategic and economic effort was needed to meet the American initiative. Gorbachev recognized the inability of the Soviet Union to deal economically with the Cold War and finally, from a combination of several factors, the USSR disintegrated. We can safely surmise that the space defense initiative was a decisive factor in the breakup of the Soviet Union. What I believe motivates Putin is the ambition to restore Russia to what it was in the past, when it was at the highest level of world powers."

"It isn't clear to me what the connection is between what happened years ago during the Cold War and Russia's moves today, with its significant support for Iran," Deutsch persisted.

"What is clear to us today is the effect of Trump's decision to withdraw the United States from the nuclear agreement of the six powers with Iran. Russia, along with the other powers that signed the nuclear agreement with Iran remain committed to the agreement. At the same time as canceling our participation, Trump imposed additional economic sanctions to try to bring Iran to its knees, but this didn't happen. Another element of pressure was the assassination of General Soleimani, commander of the Quds Force. We believe Iran will not give up on an appropriate response. We're still waiting for a substantial attack against us and against Israel. It is important to remember how strong Soleimani's influence was on the formation of a predominantly Shiite front in the Middle East. A key country for the Iranian strategy he developed is Syria, but we cannot underestimate Russia's presence in what is going on in Syria."

"That's all the time we'll spend on the background reviews, which were extremely helpful," intervened the assistant secretary, "but now it's important we hear the core of the problem."

"Of course, General Dayton, I'll get to it right away. Putin, the autocratic Russian President has decided to prioritize assisting Bashar al-Assad in his war against the rebels. In this framework, he has provided advanced weapon systems such as S-300 missiles. The Russians' intention by doing this is to ensure the continued stationing of the Russian Navy's ships in the port city of Tartus in the northwest of the country. Putin is aware of Iran's policy to assure Assad's remaining in power. Russia also makes sure to maintain contact with Israel. Putin knows how to hold both ends of the stick. Iran continues to deviate from the nuclear agreement on the grounds that the United States is no longer part of it and the more troubling thing is Putin's decision to allow Iran to move forward with the development of nuclear weapons. According to Iran's policy – as we learned from the words of the Iranian supreme leader – this would be an appropriate response to the murder of Soleimani, and the damage to the enrichment facilities at the centrifuge plant in Natanz and other nuclear research sites.

"It seems like an unusual move," commented Deutsch. "To the best of my recollection, Russia and Ukraine did not transfer any information or materials on the nuclear weapon. After the dissolution of the Soviet Union, you arranged generous funding to enable nuclear scientists from both countries to engage in research and not offer their expertise to entities seeking shortcuts to obtaining nuclear weapons."

"That's right." confirmed the assistant secretary, "It's essential that we find out exactly what Iran is doing to develop the weapon. Whether it's only Iranian scientists – whose ability should not be underestimated – or, God help us, unconditional assistance from Russian and Ukrainian nuclear scientists."

"We have to remember, Doctor Deutsch," continued the research officer, "that the Iranians prepared extremely well for a cyber-battle after the 'Stuxnet' worm damaged the uranium enrichment centrifuges at the Natanz enrichment plant. They responded with a fast-tracked development to enable them to use cyber for attack and for defense."

"North Korea is responsible for the technological assistance in cyber. We have seen proof of their capabilities in the cyberattacks on water and energy facilities in the United States and Israel. Our connections with the intelligence communities in Israel also bolster our information base on the alarming progress in supersonic missile technology Russia has decided to give to Iran."

"To Iran? That's highly advanced strategic technology. We're not even there yet." added Deutsch. "Where did that come from? What else do you know, Thomas?

"The ultrasonic communication was picked up by Israeli intelligence and only recently passed on to us," answered the deputy minister. "In this area, too, Deutsch, we are counting on your solid relationship with the Mossad and the research team that Nahari is leading," concluded the assistant secretary. "We can use your help in getting the most out of the intelligence and technology of our two countries. I suggest you take time today for an up-to-date and detailed briefing of the information gathered by the FBI thus far – and then we will discuss how to move forward from there."

Chapter 7

STANFORD

Their morning coffee was a tradition at Dan and Noam's house before starting out for another day of challenges and stress at the Ofek Hadad Company, and at the university. This time it was a little different. Dan told Noam that Dr. Deutsch had invited them to a lunch meeting. "What does Deutsch want to update us on?" Noam wondered as she poured the morning coffee "Why does he want me to be with you at the meeting? I hope this won't interfere with the academic and commercial activities we finally got going."

"I don't know much more than you do, Nono. It might just be about his meetings at the Pentagon. In any case, we know Deutsch wouldn't call us in for no reason. No need to start guessing, we'll know soon enough what went on at the Pentagon."

"Stanford's SRI is considered to be the crown jewel of academic research. This is to a large extent thanks to the professional level and enthusiastic creativity of carefully recruited young researchers. Ben Ari spent two years as a senior research fellow there, and he developed a solid working and personal relationship with Deutsch when he was the director. SRI's involvement in the war against Iranian terrorism and Deutsch's active participation began during that period."

***

"Good morning Dan, Noam," Deutsch greeted the young couple with a smile on his face. "Thank you for your vigilance and for raising the alarm about the threat of deepfake. We heard from the NSA about the fake video conversation between former President Obama and the Iranian foreign minister."

"Noam exposed the phony clip. We're eager to hear more details and we also want to know what we can do, assuming that this one is only the beginning of deepfake on the international level," said Dan, who did not conceal his pride in Noam's professional attentiveness.

"Right you are, Dan," Deutsch responded. "In the meantime, I received further information on my visit to Washington. NSA is almost certain that the Obama fake is the work of the Russians. They say that this is a typical move by Putin and is likely a response to the sanctions levied by the United States and the European Union over Russia's aggressive moves against Ukraine, especially after the takeover of the Crimean Peninsula on the coast of the Black Sea."

"That's all very interesting," said Noam. "What do you think Dan and I can do?"

"Easy does it," Deutsch tried to reassure them. "I am getting to the heart of a new threat, different from

Russia's previous involvement. It's about the strengthening of its ties with Iran. Iran's relations with Russia and North Korea comprise a threatening nuclear triangle. Noam, you correctly pointed out the importance of advanced technologies in the war on terrorism. We will get to that later. First, I want to fill you in on what I heard from members of the special research team that began operations on the subterranean floor of the Pentagon. I assume you're aware of Russia's menacing transfer of supersonic missile technology to Iran. This is a highly unusual move by the Russians, to share advanced technology with a foreign country. These missiles, which we ourselves have not yet completely developed, are faster than Mach five. They're also long-range and pose a real threat to the United States, particularly because they cannot be detected by currently known defensive means. What's your take on this, Dan?

"It's a serious problem. We'll need special research teams both at headquarters and in industry. The Iranians have just started developing their own version of the supersonic missiles, but it won't be long before they can produce them."

Noam spoke up, "I understand that during your meetings at the Pentagon, you discussed in depth the issue of Russia's recent threatening moves. In the discussions at the Pentagon was there a call for Israeli inclusion? Can you share anything more with us? After all, this definitely concerns us as well." Noam would not let Deutsch off the hook when she felt there was something he was not telling them.

"Yes, definitely. The assistant secretary of defense told me something significant and threatening; if it is true...the existence of an espionage network, much bigger than the Pollard affair. The FBI believes Israel is involved in its operation."

Dan and Noam were silent. They looked intently at Deutsch in an attempt to interpret and digest this piece of information. Deutsch waited several moments before continuing. "In the Pentagon team's summary report, we recommended keeping Israel updated and sharing information with them. The assistant secretary asked the head of the CIA to contact the Mossad chief, and this has already been done. You and Dan are recognized by all the security forces as top-secret partners in these areas and therefore I can inform you as to what's happening."

"Israel will cooperate fully with our closest ally," said Dan. "What do we do here and now?"

"At the moment, there is no need to burden you with things that would interfere with your routine. You have a lot going on in your company dealing with the new threat of high-speed missiles. Dan, and Noam, you also have your academic research."

"Deutsch, Noam is making excellent progress in the derivatives of Artificial Intelligence technology," Dan tried to return to the subject that most interested him and Noam. He mentioned the research conducted by Noam as part of her doctorate in the field of face recognition and later in her postdoc when she developed an algorithm for interpreting facial expressions. "Noam has many unanswered questions to resolve," continued

Dan, "maybe she can tell us what she needs to make further progress."

"I feel I'm on the threshold of something big that connects perfectly with face recognition technology. I'm talking about deepfake. The little I know about it is its connection to computer vision. I'm certain, Dutch, that your institute is involved in research activity in all applications of Artificial Intelligence?"

"That's true, Noam, like many other research institutes around the world, we are studying Artificial Intelligence and technologies that stem from it. The roots of academic research into deepfake technology are mainly in the area of computer vision. Initially, researchers focused on computerized processing of digital images and videos. The program could change existing video clips of a person speaking and synchronize it with a different audio track. What is relevant to you, Noam, is the capability to change facial expressions completely automatically. This is done using machine learning techniques, another product of Artificial Intelligence, which made the connection between the voice produced by a character in the video and the movements and facial expressions. One of the most prominent researchers in the fields of Artificial Intelligence and the technologies that developed from them is known to you..."

"And who is that?" asked Noam.

"A young scientist named Dr. Eric Grossfeld, a graduate of the University of Berlin. He recently joined our institute as a post-doctoral fellow..."

"He's already here?" Dan continued and asked, "Wow, great!"

"Yes, Eric, the son of Doctor Dieter Grossfeld," confirmed Deutsch with a wink at Nimer and Hassan's new identities. "Eric received excellent recommendations for acceptance at the institute and I know that you both were among those who recommended him. He is with us as a postdoctoral research fellow on Artificial Intelligence technologies. I am sure Eric justifies the opinions that made it possible for him to be admitted to the institute. And Noam, you will find him an impressive scholar and a fascinating conversationalist."

At that point, Deutsch called Eric and asked him to join the meeting.

***

"Eric, I thought, it would be good for you to meet with Dan and Noam, who are among the few who know the whole story of you and your father. Your doctorate studies at the University of Berlin and the honors you earned, including the university president's medal, impressed all of us. I have no doubt the institute will benefit from your research on Artificial Intelligence," Deutsch complimented him. "This is precisely why, my young friends, that I wanted to bring you together. The institute is home to you, Eric, and you, Dan and Noam. You have the opportunity to deal with the most confidential issues. Our shielded discussion room is at your disposal. You can already move in there and I recommend that you do so."

***

Deutsch accompanied the young people to the door of the secret and electronically shielded discussion room. Deutsch had to enter three separate codes: a password of letters and numbers, a fingerprint, and a retina scan verification. He directed their attention to the coffee area in the corner of the room and told them not to hesitate to ask him anything if needed.

Eric turned to Dan and Noam. "I join you both in valuing everything Dr. Deutsch does at the institute. And thank you for your recommendation for my post-doctorate work here. The way of working at SRI is very different from the German academic approach. The openness and flexibility I enjoy here – and this is true for all the researchers at the institute, and certainly in the United States as a whole – are distinctly different from what I experienced at the University of Berlin."

"I learned a great deal about the military history of Germany in World War II as part of my studies for a Doctor of Science degree," said Deutsch. "It is incredible how Germany was able to gather the economic resources, develop the technological expertise, and above all have the human know-how to achieve what they did: the assault rifle copied by the Russians, who call it the Kalashnikov, the anti-tank RPG, encrypted communications, the jet engine in the Messer-Schmidt and especially the V1 and V2 rockets, all phenomenal examples of German scientific military achievements. It's an impressive history and we remember how the United States on one side, and the Soviet Union on the other, both fought for control of the German military-industrial complex. The United States gained knowledge of long-range missile technology and the Soviet Union got the assault rifle, the RPG launcher and other products," continued Deutsch in his historical overview, "but today, Eric, because of Artificial Intelligence, we are in a completely different kind of world. Noam, you're well acquainted with deepfake, how can you help us," asked Deutsch.

For a moment, Noam hesitated, perhaps thinking how best to succinctly present what she had achieved in the research on facial expressions and especially how to tie it into the field of deepfake.

"Deepfake definitely aligns with facial recognition – I dealt with it in my doctorate and in my further research in interpretation of facial expressions. However, I am not familiar with the computer program that takes existing video clips of a person speaking and synchronizes his expressions with a different audio track. Dan, from what I heard from you, this is done with 'machine learning,' which makes a connection between the voice in the video and the shape and movements of the person's face. Now I ask you, Eric, did I explain this clearly enough? I understand that in your Ph.D. you studied in depth the various technologies that rely on Artificial Intelligence. Did you include deepfake in your research? What do you recommend we do next?"

"Thank you, Noam, for your interest and openness. Your findings in the field of facial expressions are impressive, and in fact, they are an essential condition for the advanced activation of deepfake technology," responded Eric. "You both should know, Dan and Noam, everything having to do with Artificial Intelligence has fascinated me from the day I entered the university in Berlin. That's why I chose to focus on it. It continually becomes more extensive and fascinating. During my studies for the degree, I delved into 'machine learning,' a subfield of computer science and Artificial Intelligence. Machine learning requires the development of algorithms to enable the computer to learn from examples and works on a variety of computational tasks where classical programming is not possible. I also did research in two fields parallel to machine learning: data mining and pattern recognition. Many of the tools and algorithms developed in these fields are co-shared with other developments."

"I'm certain it won't take long for you and Noam to develop applications for the technology. The challenges we face are both for security purposes as well as a rapid and powerful entry into the civilian sphere," said Dan.

Eric turned to Noam, "Based on this, I can see how easy it is to understand and connect deepfake technology to your Ph.D. research. I discovered that not long ago, a deepfake program called 'fake-up' was launched. It is animated and allows users to create and share videos with different faces relatively easily. The application uses an artificial neural network. It requires a graphics processor and relatively limited storage space to create a fake video. You still need a lot of visual material of the person whose face you want to insert into the original video for a deep learning algorithm to acquire which aspects of the image to replace. This is another addition to the toolbox of Artificial Intelligence that you work on Dan, and the facial expression technology Noam has developed."

Eric impressed Dan and Noam during their meeting in the shielded discussion room, with a complete metamorphosis into a superimposed German identity. This was reflected in his way of speaking and even in his body language. Noam could not refrain from complimenting Eric on the complete integration of his new Germanic persona.

Eric waved off the flattery with a shake of his head and a slightly embarrassed smile. He was ready to go on to the next stage. He came up with a somewhat "crazy" idea for Dan and Noam: to transmit to the Revolutionary Guard in Iran a message from Nimer in his original identity, which would create serious confusion. The result would divert those looking for Nimer away from their current concentration on finding him. Eric was going to tell them that he had already spoken about it with his father, who had agreed to the unexpected strategy.

"The idea is not so crazy, Eric, and your father's approval makes it even more feasible," Dan praised him. "I would go ahead and run some experiments in deepfake before we step it up and operate against the Iranian Revolutionary Guard."

"Dan is right, Eric. It will be more expedient for us to start with a trial experiment," said Noam. "And we can do this of course, after you study the details of the materials I have on the facial recognition projects. I suggest that we start small, and after verifying the results, we can move forward and prepare projects to deceive the Revolutionary Guard and the Quds Force, which will affect their decisions in the field."

Chapter 8

TEHRAN

Madani had full authority to use the Quds Force research team in planning a new revenge operation. General Kashani made it clear to him that this time he expected a successful, impressive operation.

Madani held a brainstorming session with experienced combat officers along with engineers and researchers familiar with the latest technologies. Madani found himself wavering between the officers' recommendations and the scientists' positions. The combat officers insisted on a major operation based on field-proven methods. The scientists, on the other hand, pressed the case for new technologies centered on cyber-based algorithms, AI and the technologies that stemmed from it. By nature, Dr. Madani was biased toward the scientists' approach, but he was concerned about the possible failure of systems that had not been field tested in previous operations. He felt confident enough to share his reservations with General Kashani.

***

"There is major disagreement between the two groups that is problematic. That is why I have come to you to present the issues that make the choice difficult."

"I am not surprised. I could have foreseen the situation, even without participating in the discussions. Our military personnel, most of whom took part in past wars against Iraq, are not known for being able to think too far ahead..."

"Correct, General Kashani. In addition, they are skeptical of what they call 'Artificial Intelligence trickery.' Computers, they passionately claim, are no match for a kilogram of explosives. And at least according to our experience so far, they are quite right...So the question is whether we are ready to give up on the use of technologies that have emerged in the environment of Artificial Intelligence, cyber defense, and attack systems...I have not heard anything new from the 'spokesmen' about explosives in missile warheads or in booby-trapped cars. Until now we have only met with failure due to the enemy's technological advantage, which has so far thwarted our plans. But at heart, commander, even a massive attack on the embassy would not compare to a spectacular operation such as the attack on the Twin Towers carried out by al-Qaeda. In addition, it is important to upgrade our defense against cyber-attacks and sustain our ability to listen in on enemy networks. It is a vital component of any communications system to function in the future."

"I remember Dr. Nimer Al-Khaldi's impression after his visit to North Korea's Cyber University. You were also there and reported on the wise decision of Kim

Jong-il, the previous ruler of North Korea, to establish such an institution. Many years ago he foresaw that the future battlefield would be waged with computers and not conventional weapons. Kim Jong-il did not speak about Artificial Intelligence, of course. However, today, under the rule of his son Kim Jong-un, this extremely poor country is a world leader in Artificial Intelligence research and cyber activity led by the experts trained in the elite hacking program at Mirim College in the military academy."

"Yes, Commander, that is so, and they have made many technological achievements such as the long-range missiles with precision warheads and defense against discovery of tunnels, which is vital to Hezbollah in Lebanon and to Hamas in the Gaza Strip. But above all, there is progress towards nuclear weapons. They have advanced despite all efforts of the Western powers to stop them and have thus assured the safety of the North Korean regime."

"I understand, Madani, that this issue did not come up at all in the discussions you held, and the subject of uranium enrichment at our plant in Natanz was not mentioned. The nuclear issue is in a different league, isn't it? I remember that Dr. Nimer al-Khaldi was enthusiastic about North Korea after being invited to observe an underground nuclear test. I am convinced that the North Koreans will allow you to be present at such a test. Perhaps it would be good to get off the 'conventional explosives vs. Artificial Intelligence' debate and consider focusing on nuclear weapons. This could also be a strong response to the onerous sanctions that the president of the United States recently added to the list."

"If we concentrate on the area we were engaged in at the brainstorming session I held, Commander, I thought I would formulate an integrated summary of the positions we identified at the end of that discussion. As such, I recommend leaving the option of conventional weapons systems on the table. We will go by President Putin's directive and will not reveal anything about the ultrasonic missiles except to the few top-secret partners we've decided on."

"That seems to me worthy of being presented to the supreme leader for the large scale operation. I am sure he will support it and instruct us to formulate it," added General Kashani, with obvious enthusiasm.

"At the same time," Madani added, "I would not give up on the effort to upgrade our ability to manage defense and attack systems in cyber technology. I recommend entrusting the preparations for the use of the ultrasonic missile systems to the officers who were fighters in the past and whom we have chosen to share the secret of our high-speed missile program. On the other hand, operations that rely on Artificial Intelligence should be assigned to the team of young researchers who work with me on the technological issues related to AI."

"Your recommendation, Dr. Madani, seems a good one, and appropriate. Present it to the supreme leader and emphasize that these are diversionary and back-up operations, and also that we are working on something colossal as to the targets toward which the high-speed missiles will be launched."

"Thank you, Commander. To gain the supreme leader's approval, it is important we present the responses and the preparations for their implementation. I need to go to North Korea as soon as possible. Can you give me your approval to take two or three of my young researchers with me for the visit to Pyongyang to meet with the senior hackers there?"

"That will be no problem, Madani. Choose your best people. They will acquire the latest knowledge in Artificial Intelligence technologies and we'll finally be able to upgrade our communication systems. To prepare for the meeting with the supreme leader, let's discuss the issue of nuclear weapons and North Korea's involvement in our development program. Using the most secure communication channels, we have forwarded a request to General Lee Hong-Jik to invite you to observe the upcoming test of a new, powerful nuclear warhead. We have not yet received final approval but it is pending."

"I would very much like to witness the nuclear test in North Korea. Such approval would be a step, albeit not yet binding, for major cooperation. I did not raise this possibility on my previous visit to Pyongyang when I met with General Lee Hong-Jik, but under these conditions, it will be possible for me to broach the subject."

"The supreme leader would also like to hear about something else, Madani: the entire uranium enrichment affair..."

"You mean the attack carried out at the uranium enrichment plant in Natanz? It is indeed a disturbing issue that requires us to take economic and perhaps technological steps to regain our enrichment capabilities. We must remedy the weaknesses that enabled the enemy to introduce a large quantity of explosives into the centrifuge plant. The leader has already issued a harsh statement and asked for clarification from the commander of the Revolutionary Guard. Someone in the counter-espionage division was caught off guard."

"Exactly. And so, Doctor Madani, we should be thankful for the leader's complete trust in the Quds Force, even after General Soleimani's demise. I must stress that it is your obligation to prepare a comprehensive and convincing review to reassure the leader. I don't need to remind you of the good relationship that exists with the Pakistani scientist, Dr. Abdul Qadir Khan, who will be able to assist us in getting the Natanz enrichment plant back into operation. I also think it is worthwhile to bring up another topic that can help us get past this crisis." Kashani hastened to clarify, "I am talking about our need for Russia's support precisely at this critical strategic junction."

"You are right about needing Russia's goodwill, but what leads you to believe they will actively support our development of nuclear weapons? We remember their assistance in completing the construction and operation of the power reactors at the site near Bushehr. Their willingness to receive the nuclear fuel rods of the reactors after their terms of cooperation were over is proof of their goodwill. And it is true that we assist them in supporting Syria – important strategically under Assad – and through them also in support of Hezbollah. But Commander, what guarantee is there that they will aid us on the issue of nuclear weapons? They have never passed essential information on to any other country."

"True, we have no precedent in which Russia transmitted precise information about the construction of nuclear weapons. Another source would be scientists from countries with nuclear facilities dating back to the former Soviet Union and who may be competition for the Russians. As long as the information comes to us without the other side knowing about it, we may benefit from the option and the competition. The most likely aid would come from granting permits, perhaps clandestinely, to nuclear scientists in other countries who have become redundant."

"Very well, Commander, I will include that idea in the review that I'll prepare for the leader."

"Ah...you should also consult with the professor who is the director of nuclear development here, and see what he has to say about this, and perhaps also what can be expected from our friends in North Korea. I remember you telling me the professor was in favor of your visit to North Korea and the possibility of observing the upcoming nuclear weapons test."

***

Madani was tense as he sat in his room with the laptop, reviewing the notes from the brainstorming session. He felt the weight of preparing the review for the leader bearing down on his shoulders. He tried to recall and examine step by step the ideas that were put forward. He had no problem formulating the recommendations of the officers who insisted that any response be based on combat-proven weapon systems. The notes on Artificial Intelligence and cyber technology were clear to him and he knew exactly how to present them in the review for the leader. In fact, both these two areas as possibilities for revenge operations were already included in a draft he had prepared. However, this was not the major issue for General Kashani. Madani thought to himself: "I must devote considerable time to the nuclear program. The professor, the director of nuclear research, is the best source and I hope he will agree to lend me his wisdom and experience..." He asked his secretary to arrange an urgent meeting with the director of research activities related to nuclear weapons.

***

"Hello Doctor Madani. Good to see you again," said the professor. He rose from his chair to shake Madani's hand as he entered the small, simply furnished office at the university. "I understand you have a pressing matter to discuss," said the professor as he took Madani's arm and led him to a chair. "How can I help?"

"Professor, I am preparing a document for the supreme leader. It includes recommendations for actions in retaliation for the heinous damage inflicted upon us by the United States and Israel, the Great Satan and the Little Satan. You know, Professor, better than any of us, the intensity and significance of the harm done by these two demon nations. Our response in my humble opinion must be retribution of a strength that has not been seen until now. At the same time, I believe there should also be continued activity on the development of nuclear weapons in the very face of our enemies. Is this your understanding also? Is it not too complex after the nuclear agreement between us and the six powers was invalidated by the American president? I remember that you recommended a return to the development of nuclear weapons, but carefully and without having it exposed if possible. The other question is: Can we complete the development alone or is assistance required from a friendly nuclear power? And is this even plausible?"

"Indeed, my young friend, the issue is complex and requires measured and careful steps if we wish to achieve significant advancement. We all remember the decision in 2003 to stop the development of nuclear weapons. We even made certain to transmit this message via the Swiss ambassador, as a trusted intermediary to the president of the United States. The truth is, Dr. Madani, we never completely stopped research on the theoretical aspects of nuclear weapons. At the same time, and with the knowledge of the International Atomic Energy Agency, IAEA, based in Vienna, we were engaged in the establishment of a uranium enrichment plant near Natanz. Harassment at this plant began with a cyberattack with the software worm 'Stuxnet.' That was long before we began discussions for the agreement with the six powers. We had an incentive to adhere to the terms of the agreement because in return, the onerous sanctions of the United

States and the European Union were lifted. Now, after Trump's decision to withdraw the United States from the agreement, we have a good reason to continue the uranium enrichment process and the development of nuclear weapons."

"It is clear, Professor, that thanks to Trump we were given the freedom to act without the limitations that the agreement with the six powers imposed upon us. I also assume that we will not allow ourselves to unnecessarily reveal that we are continuing to make progress in our development of nuclear weapons. Such admission would result in international pressure and possibly even more burdensome sanctions. But don't we need outside help? What is the right thing to do in order to receive such assistance? Will Russia be able to take on this task? Russia is our ally in many areas: the fight against al-Qaeda, assisting Assad in Syria and Hezbollah in Lebanon, and it also allied with China to help North Korea become a nuclear power. Or do you think we do not need outside assistance?"

Madani held his breath and waited for the reply of the professor, who was in no hurry to respond. Did I overdo it with my questions? Did I stop the professor's willingness to share with me the policy he was following? Madani hesitated and decided to wait patiently for the professor to speak, which he finally did:

"I would continue the good relations you have with North Korea. I supported your trip to Pyongyang and the likelihood of your being invited to the upcoming nuclear test. I have been in contact with General Lee Hong-Jik in recent years and I know he has a high opinion of your abilities. Your visit will be full of important issues. In my opinion, the right moment to broach the subject of aid to our nuclear programs will be immediately after the nuclear test – assuming it is successful," said the professor, who avoided mentioning Russia. "If you are free in the coming days before the trip to Pyongyang, I would be happy to make available to you the head of our research department who will broaden your knowledge on the latest developments in the nuclear field."

"I would be most glad to learn from him and be more prepared for my visit to North Korea," said Madani as he took leave of the professor with an extraordinarily positive feeling and a warm, prolonged handshake.

Chapter 9

TEL AVIV

"We have disturbing new information from the Evyatar team," said Nahari, before Gideon had time to take his seat in the conference room. "It's clear, Gideon, that the Iranians are preparing a devastating revenge attack for the operations that we and the United States have recently carried out. I asked Evyatar and his team to fill us in on the details. Let's hear from them."

"First of all, I am happy to report that we were able to overcome the cyber threats Iran carried out, probably with North Korean assistance," said Evyatar. "All communications were cut off for 24 hours. Just a little while ago, we were able to crack the sophisticated algorithm with the help of our NSA partners in the American embassy here in Tel Aviv,

"Congratulations," cut in Nahari, "and what have you learned? What is the new threat?"

"We found a complex combination of several elements that we have not seen before. One area, as expected, deals with the revenge operation not yet carried out for the assassination of Soleimani, the former commander of the Quds Force. There was a sweeping recommendation from top administration officials in Tehran not to be content with an attack on an embassy or on a central economic facility within the United States. The foreign minister and the Iranian president wanted an action that would continue Soleimani's policy of strengthening ties with friendly countries and expanding Iran's control in the Middle East and the entire world. We haven't picked up anything clear about the plans for revenge in the Iranian media..."

"That's not surprising," Gideon interjected, "the question is not 'what' they do but 'how.' Have you identified in which direction they're heading?"

"It is important to point out," Evyatar went on, "that Soleimani visited Syria as part of their support for Bashar Assad in his war against the rivals that threaten his regime. He visited Lebanon and met with Nasrallah to strengthen ties with Hezbollah. Soleimani then went on to meetings in Syria before flying his executive jet to Iraq. The relationship with Syria that Soleimani was able to build was necessary to support Hezbollah, Iran's loyal envoy in the region, and to strengthen Iran's overall presence in the Middle East. The former commander of the Quds Force was concerned about the presence of agents of the United States and Israel in Syria, Iraq, and even inside Iran. After the latest attacks, Iran claims that these agents also facilitated the assassination of the nuclear research professor. Another issue is Russia's role in the region. Putin is playing a double game here. On one hand, he unhesitatingly supports Bashar al-Assad's regime and turns a blind eye to Iran's increasing presence in Syria, and on the other, he maintains direct contact with Israel, and especially with the Israeli prime minister, and does not interfere in Israel's air force attacks on Iranian military targets on Syrian soil."

"Let's be clear, Evyatar, what is the connection between the Russian policy in our region and Iran's response to the series of operations we recently imposed on it," asked Nahari. "It is clear, of course, that Syria wants to keep the port facility in Tartus open to the Russian fleet in the Mediterranean and this can explain the unreserved Russian support for the Assad regime."

"I'm getting to that, Nahari," Evyatar hastened to reply, "you'll hear in a moment about the ties between Russia and Iran on nuclear issues and how they connect to Iran's intentions to respond to the vulnerability of their scientists and nuclear facilities, in light of the attack on the uranium enrichment centrifuge facility in Natanz. Let me say right from the beginning," continued Evyatar, pointing to the two young men with him, "that the Russian speakers in my team have already accumulated many hours of listening in on communications between Russia and Iran..."

"You can also receive significant support from the Russian group operating in the IDF, part of the Russian group established in the Intelligence Division in Unit 8200," added Nahari, "I will update the head of Intelligence today while you continue looking into Russia's role."

"Russia's involvement in the region is multi-faceted and long-term," Evyatar went on. "In the nuclear field, we need to remember that Russia came to the rescue to complete the construction of the nuclear power plant in Bushehr. The design of the reactor and the initial construction was by Siemens, the German company. They undertook to build two reactors at a site located east of the city of Bushehr. International pressure, mainly American, resulted in Germany's withdrawal from the project. Russia took over the project and completed the construction of the first reactor in Bushehr. Today, Russia is continuing, with a contract to build eight additional reactors near Bushehr. We have to note that Russia receives the nuclear fuel rods that have finished their role in electricity production. They do this to prevent Iran from producing the plutonium created in the fuel rods during the process. Russia was an active partner and supported Iran's positions in the negotiations on the nuclear agreement with the six JCPOA powers led by President Obama. Trump withdrew America from the agreement, creating a situation where Iran is not explicitly committed to the agreement but respects the decision of the five remaining powers. Iran has resumed acting very cautiously in the nuclear field in anticipation of the change of power in the United States."

"We all remember what happened after the breakup of the Soviet Union," Gideon broke in. "The United States and the Western countries were worried that the unemployed nuclear scientists would be available to countries wanting to take a significant shortcut in acquiring nuclear weapon capability. To the best of my knowledge, neither Russia nor Ukraine leaked any nuclear weapons secrets. It may be easier for us to track Iran's progress than to penetrate Russia's cyber defenses. However, it is important to note that we've created one loophole of information about nuclear weapons and aid thereof from North Korea. We don't yet have a complete picture, but it is certain that Iran aims to return to full development activity of nuclear weapons and it expects assistance from Russia. Putin could turn a blind eye to 'volunteer' nuclear scientists who do not play a role in Russia's nuclear system today."

"All right, Evyatar, you have a lot of hard work ahead. We won't hold you back. Get going!"

***

"It sounds threatening to me," said Gideon when he and Nahari were left alone in the office. "I will keep working on this and give you my assessments in a day or two. If it turns out that the situation requires reinforcement of Evyatar's team, I recommend that you put your trust in the young people who have already proven their abilities. In my opinion, Dr. Dieter Grossfeld and I ought to remain as experienced consultants, along with Eric, Dieter's son. Dan, Noam, and Evyatar can deal with the new threats."

Chapter 10

TEHRAN

General Kashani, commander of the Quds Force, called a situation assessment meeting as part of his taking office. He stated his concern about the repeated attacks on the Iranian forces that help protect the Alawite regime and especially the Syrian president. Kashani had spoken of this to Doctor Madani at a preparatory meeting between the two following another assassination of a nuclear scientist. North Korea, which a few years before had helped build the nuclear reactor near Deir ez-Zor emphasized Kashani, is claiming that there was no proper response to the destruction of the reactor, carried out by Israel with the support of the United States. The general also asked for an update on the status of Iran's nuclear weapons development and asked Madani to have a group of experts attend the meeting.

"Greetings, and thank you for participating in this important discussion," began General Kashani. "I have requested to hold this assessment of the situation after the series of events that have severely affected the continuation of our activities in the region. Doctor Madani will open the meeting and present the topics for discussion. Dr. Madani, you have all of our attention." ordered the general.

Madani began: "The despicable assassination of the professor director of nuclear development, just a few days ago, is disturbing both because of the failure of our intelligence to forewarn us of the preparations, and our inability to protect the man who led the entire nuclear development program. Furthermore, we were shocked to learn that the enemy was able to get their hands on a secret archive documenting our nuclear activity over many years, up until 2003. They stole the archive from right under our noses. The culprits have not yet been found, and the archive is now in Israeli hands. They probably shared the details with the United States as well. Another area and a source of great concern is the explosion the enemy perpetrated in the uranium enrichment facility near Natanz. We must also add to the sequence of failures the tests of arrowheads for the long-range missiles. It is a failure that leaves us with a broken trough in a strategic area of great importance to us. There is no doubt that our situation requires a supreme effort to improve in all the areas I mentioned. Of course, the supreme leader is aware of all this and he urges us to use all our abilities to overcome these crises. I suggest, General Kashani, that we now hear from Intelligence personnel, and then from the head of the nuclear development program. It is essential we be briefed on the current state of development and ways to speed it up."

"Thank you, Madani," said General Kashani as he

turned to the head of the intelligence division of the Quds Force who took a long pause before speaking about the division's failures and offering a series of apologies. Not only did the intelligence of the Quds Force not avert the enemy's operations, but also the entire information organization of the Revolutionary Guards was responsible for the failures.

"It is unpleasant and troubling to hear such difficult things, but one must not run away to an imaginary universe where all is well," ruled General Kashani. "We must face reality and strive for profound changes in our intelligence network. Let us now hear the new director of nuclear research and development. Professor? We are all waiting to hear from you!"

***

"I will not reveal any secrets to you that you did not know about, even if not in detail." the director of nuclear research began, "In 2003, after the Second Gulf War, when Saddam Hussein was overthrown by a coalition led by the United States, we decided to freeze the development of nuclear weapons. The weapons unit underwent the necessary conversion for academic research and uranium enrichment activity, with the warm support of the Pakistani scientist Abdul-Qadir Khan. It continued without interruption. We also went on with activity at the military base in Parchin, where we conducted research on special materials. The logic was that these might help us when we get back to developing nuclear weapons. We did not make sufficient progress, specifically due to negotiations on our agreement with the six powers to significantly stop all nuclear activity." The professor paused for a moment and scrutinized his listeners. He saw from their expressions and full attention that it was possible to go on. "Our agreement with the six powers included canceling construction of the major research reactor in Arak, which was intended to produce plutonium. Shortly after the agreement was signed, we fitted the reactor with a different core than the one originally planned for it. As for the research personnel, I am sorry to say that the interruption of research activity has severely weakened our capabilities. Many researchers retired, others who had gained experience were assassinated – and we know who was responsible for that... The remaining small number of staff rested on the broad shoulders of the martyred professor."

"And what happens now, professor? We are all aware of the supreme leader's direct order to include the development of nuclear weapons in the framework of the 'Great Revenge.' How do we go about this, with the wisdom and great experience of the Shahid professor no longer available to us?"

"There is no doubt that we need real help from a country that has already developed nuclear weapons. North Korea can be a good source for that. In recent years, a special relationship has developed between the professor and General Dr. Lee Hong-Jik, who is in charge of technological development in North Korea. Dr. Madani, who recently met the general during his visit to Pyongyang, can testify to the appreciation and admiration that existed in the technological community of North Korea thanks to the late professor."

"I can testify, General Kashani, to the special status the late professor had gained following his scientific assistance for the development of a variety of new technologies in North Korea, especially in the nuclear field. I am sure that the newly appointed professor, who was his deputy until recently, is also highly regarded. I definitely would like to accompany the professor to Pyongyang for meetings with General Lee and the top research and development people there," Madani stated.

"And what about contact with Russia?" asked General Kashani, "Do you think it is possible to use the important strategic relationship between us to receive support in the nuclear field?"

"I am sure the Russians will agree to the visit of the professor who is the director of our nuclear development program," Madani replied, "and I will be happy to join him. The Russians are responsible, as we all know, for completing the construction of the nuclear power plants near Bushehr and they also took it upon themselves to receive and store the nuclear fuel after it completed its role in the production of electricity."

"What do you say, esteemed professor, about Doctor Madani's recommendations? Are we burdening you with tasks that will make it more difficult for you in managing the technological development in such a challenging period? Will you have time for the round of visits that might take us on a new path?" Kashani was careful not to apply too much pressure.

"General Kashani, I have no doubt that the visits

Madani mentioned should be held. However, we must remember that the nuclear field is the most highly sensitive of all technologies and not to expect too much, even though it would be good to rely on the strong ties we have there. We also should remember that North Korea could not have reached its position among the top nuclear powers without China's initial push. Today, China is more cautious and does not offer friendly nations aid in the nuclear field."

"Well, gentlemen, thank you for your information on the progress in the nuclear issue and the path we now need to follow."

Chapter 11

PYONGYANG

A small number of passengers sat aboard the outdated Russian Antonov aircraft of North Korea's national airline. When the plane took off from Beijing, Madani saw it as his duty to reassure the young engineers with him that the plane would land safely at Pyongyang airport. North Korea's national airline enjoyed no special budgetary privilege. The economic pressure of the West on North Korea, an embargo that included a ban on the sale of American or European aircraft contributed to lack of modernization. After a shaky, sputtering landing, the plane stopped and the young people breathed a sigh of relief. Two old model limousines were waiting by the plane. Next to them stood a beautiful young North Korean woman who Madani remembered from his previous visit. "Welcome to North Korea," the young woman called out in a playful voice, "I am Dr. Sun Mei from the Public Relations Department of our security services. How good to see you again, Doctor Madani. I am glad to see you came with professional staff. Welcome!"

"Hello Doctor Sun Mei. I am glad we are meeting again," Madani replied, "We are pleased to be your guests, and look forward to the important meetings you have arranged for us."

"First, we are going to the Koryo Hotel, our official guest hotel that you probably remember, Doctor Madani," Sun Mei updated the newcomers, and the cars began the journey on their way to the city center.

"Here is the file with the meeting program we have prepared for you. Sun-Mei said to Madani. "Please see if the topics need to be changed or if anything needs to be added. Let me know if you find everything suitable after you review the file. In the meantime, I can tell you that General Lee Hong-Jik, in charge of technological research and development, is looking forward to meeting you and your team tomorrow morning. We will arrive at the hotel in about half an hour, and in the meantime, you can enjoy the views of this beautiful city of ours." Madani glanced from time to time at the landscape that unfolded before his eyes. She pointed out the statues and the huge monument on the hill with the impressive, sculpted figures of Kim Il Sung, the patriarch of the nation, and the current leader, Kim Jong-un. The cars continued, passing under the massive triumphal arch of Pyongyang. Madani thanked the efficient escort, but he was more interested in the plan of the visit than the landscape. He looked through the file page by page and was surprised by the quantity of topics that were awaiting him. Sun Mei decided not to burden him with any more touristic information.

***

The hotel was in the center of the city. "For you, Dr. Madani, we reserved the suite you stayed in during your previous visit and have reserved the upgraded rooms for the rest of your team." Son Mei hardly lingered at the reception desk before parting.

Madani reminded his people that the Koreans forbid unescorted tours of the city by foreign guests, without exception. "This is how the leaders make sure that its guests receive only positive information and Allah forbid they will not be exposed to the extreme hardships of the citizens," Madani explained to his staff members when they were gathered for a briefing in his suite. When he excused the others and they went to their rooms, Madani noted that the suite was well prepared according to Sun Mei's instructions, and included a basket of tropical fruits, and a refrigerator full of refreshments. Madani walked to the window from where he could see the spectacular, 170-meter high Juche Tower, built in honor of Kim Il-sung on his seventieth birthday and the Kim Il-Sung square where the annual military parades were held. Feeling tired from the long journey, Madani lay down on the spacious bed and was soon asleep.

***

The next morning, an impressive scene greeted Madani and his team at the Pungye-ri Nuclear Test Site in the north of the country. Hundreds of soldiers were positioned at the intersections and at the entrance leading to the huge buildings of the Directorate of Technological Projects. Everyone sensed that something unusual was about to take place, although only a few knew the details. General Dr. Lee Hong-Jik, the director of technological projects, stood tense and nervous at the entrance of the building where the control room for the nuclear experiments was located. The general was informed that the supreme leader, Kim Jong-un, was on his way to the test site. He waited impatiently, full of apprehension. Outwardly, the general displayed confidence and calm, but he knew that the results of the test were critical to North Korea's reputation and his head could be on the chopping block should it go wrong.

The general had established himself as far back as the days of the father of the supreme leader, and his men trembled in his presence. More than on one occasion, he had sent men to a detention camp for a minor mistake. General Dr. Lee's status was thanks to his successful development of long-range missiles based on information from North Korea's loyal friend, China. Technological knowledge also came from the Soviet Union, but achieving high-quality production of the missiles led to lucrative sales to many other countries. General Dr. Lee accomplished this at the very beginning of his career. However, few people knew that an Iranian scientist known only as "The Professor," was the real source of the technological leap on nuclear issues.

A glass partition in the control room separated the scientists who sat at computer screens and followed the progress of the countdown of the experiment.

Along with them were a few fortunate invited guests, privileged to view the experiment. Doctor Madani sat in a place of honor in the front row and listened to the English translation of Doctor Sun Mei's words. "We are all on alert," whispered Sun Mei, "our supreme leader will arrive soon, so it is clear that the countdown has almost come to an end. May the experiment be successful and impress you."

Madani saw all the scientists at the control screens suddenly leap to their feet and stand at rigid attention. The spectators also quickly stood up. Kim Jong-un's entrance into the control room was electric, causing everything to jump. A cushioned royal chair decorated with gold was placed in the center of the room for him. The ruler sat down after shaking General Lee's hand and ordered him to proceed.

The experiment went well and was soon over, an obvious success.

***

Madani had made notes and rushed to the airport for his next stop on the multi-destination trip – Beirut. He would write up his conclusions and impressions of the experiment during the fifteen-hour flight to the Middle East...

Chapter 12

BEIRUT AND TEL AVIV

Hassan Nasrallah convened the top echelon of Hezbollah to discuss the crisis. He introduced Dr. Madani, who had just arrived to provide an update on the Iranian government's assessments of the political and military situation in the region. But mainly, noted Nasrallah, the secretary General, he was there to discuss the difficult economic situation of Lebanon. Nasrallah told the gathering that Iran had appointed Dr. Madani to participate in the deliberations of "where the organization was heading" in the face of the threat of Israel, which was supported by the Americans. But, added Nasrallah, Madani would mainly be the point person in formulating a solution to the economic crisis threatening the stability of Lebanon.

"Thank you, Mr. Secretary General, for the kind words," Madani began, "I represent the Iranian Republic and bring you the blessings of our supreme leader. I undertake to assist you as much as I can – both for your security against the Israeli and American enemies; and to help Lebanon out of the disastrous economic situation. Even for us in Iran, the economic situation is not an easy one. We will have to find creative ways to give the citizens, both ours and yours, a reasonable standard of living."

"Sir, the great nation of Iran has resources that we in Lebanon can only dream about." the commander of the military branch stressed, "What power do we have in the economic sphere?"

"I do not have an immediate answer for you, Honorable Commander of the Military Branch," Madani replied, "I believe a team of experts should be appointed. I am ready to join the discussions with you, in order to identify promising courses of action. The general direction, if you ask my opinion, would be to restore calm to Lebanon and reach the level you had achieved in the past with tourism and foreign investment."

"Doctor Madani is right," Nasrallah cut in, "and you, the commander of the military arm, please stay in your area of expertise. We value the assistance your military provided to Syrian President Hafez al-Assad and his government in the war against the rebels. And in this you surely helped Iran to strengthen its influence in the region." stated Nasrallah and then turned to Madani, "Perhaps it would be possible for a special financial grant, even just to start the process of recovery in Lebanon?"

"Truly the mood of the Lebanese citizens is bad. But it is possible to improve that in another way than asking for funds that are not yet available." insisted the commander.

"What do you mean?" Nasrallah curtly cut off the

general who often overstepped his authority. "What magic medicine can you devise to change the mood of the populace?"

"I was thinking, your honor, to propose the digging of an attack tunnel and a takeover, by an elite force of our fighters, of an Israeli settlement in the north of Israel. Such an operation, if we prepare it properly, could be successful," said the commander of the military arm with enthusiasm. "It will be a great source of pride for the people."

Madani did not respond immediately, but it was clear that he should not hesitate. The idea of using attack tunnels had been accepted in Iran for a long time.

"The idea put forward by the commander of the military branch, your honor, is creative and feasible," Madani said, "but this is a large and complex operation, honorable Secretary General, which must be perfected in all its details. Any mistake in planning can cause a resounding failure and make matters worse."

"I hope that you, emissary of our great friend Iran, will help us with the planning and preparations to carry out this important operation," ventured the commander of the military arm.

"Your enthusiasm. sir, is impressive but it does not diminish the need for precise planning and the careful carrying out of each step. It will be necessary to perform a simulation scenario that will resemble the real action. This is essential for success. The Quds Force will be happy to be a partner in this endeavor."

"Thank you, Doctor Madani, and thanks to Iran, our great and loyal ally." concluded Nasrallah, "We will move forward with the planning of this operation and with God's help and the help of the great Iranian nation, we will succeed!"

The young Hezbollah fighters and the commander of the military arm at their head were eager to immediately carry out the tunnel operation. The commander called the young fighters' extensive combat experience in the Syrian army fighting the rebels as 'miraculous.' Iran's Quds Force, on the other hand, thought otherwise. After Madani's clear recommendations, the members of the military arm braced themselves to carry out the preparatory drills for the operation. Madani and two of his assistants monitored the exercises carried out on a tunnel similar to the operational one, as well as a simulated attack on an abandoned village resembling the targeted settlement.

"How ready are the Hezbollah forces?" asked General Kashani during his daily conversations with Madani. "We need to reassure the supreme leader and face down the ongoing criticism from senior members of the Revolutionary Guard. I don't need to remind you where the real threat is coming from..."

"We are following the progress of the preparations, which is going well. In the meantime, based on the opinion of the commander of Hezbollah's military arm and Nasrallah himself, the Israeli target is a settlement called Ya'ara. It is a small settlement and will be easy to capture. There is an abandoned structure in the center of the settlement, a small fortress-like building. The intention is to use it as a base to control the activity in the settlement after the occupation."

There was considerable tension in the office of Nahari, head of the Mossad, when the two senior advisers, Gideon and Nimer, left the room. The two had asked Dan, Noam, and Eric to update Evyatar and his people regarding the latest findings in the communications between Lebanon and Tehran. The name of the game, they stressed, was an exercise that was still unclear. "We uncovered media with information we knew nothing about." stated Evyatar when all the guests crowded into the surveillance and communication room. "We detected a clear intention to carry out the infiltration of a force of fighters from Lebanon into Israel through an attack tunnel. Their first step will be the use of a model of the tunnel entirely on Lebanese soil. In addition to this, we know that they have built a facility resembling an Israeli settlement to be occupied by Hezbollah fighters..." Evyatar paused for a moment and thanked Deutsch for joining the meeting. "I understand that you are bringing further support for what we perceived regarding the attack tunnel."

"Just so, Evyatar. NSA personnel in Washington detected the intention to activate a special Hezbollah fighting force that plans to move into Israeli territory through a previously unknown attack tunnel and occupy an Israeli settlement on Israel's northern border.

The NSA believes that there are more tunnels that have not been discovered by you and they assess that Hezbollah, supported by Iran, is extremely serious about this, although it will take an extraordinary effort to make it possible."

"I think that the NSA assessment regarding more

attack tunnels is correct," Dieter Grossfeld joined in, "Their presence requires, in my opinion, special action to find and destroy them."

"Dieter is right," Gideon interjected, "and he is also the right man to guide the team we set up for discovering the hidden tunnels. This will of course be carried out at the same time as preparations to thwart the attack on a settlement of ours on the northern border. This is a revelation for which we as yet have no precise information. In any event, young lady and gentlemen, you have a difficult and urgent task ahead of you."

***

Madani's communications with Kashani were intercepted by Evyatar and his team. In consultation with Dan, Noam, and Eric, he preferred to follow Hezbollah's activity only passively at this juncture. Once they received exact details of the operation, Noam would activate a deepfake to disrupt the attack. According to the information Evyatar picked up, Madani had returned to Tehran and was immediately called to report to the supreme leader on the progress of preparations for the "Tunnel Operation." He received praise but was warned of the complications Hezbollah could face in implementing the plan. It was recommended that he not celebrate success just yet. The tunnel exercise was closely monitored by Nasrallah with the aid of his military wing. A Quds Force team, led by Dr. Madani, was also monitoring the preparations.

Neither Hezbollah nor the Iranians were aware of

the full surveillance Evyatar and his team were conducting. Their interception system was reinforced by Dan, Noam, and Eric in collaboration with Gideon and Dieter as advisors.

"We are taking the necessary caution required in our surveillance of the exercises," Evyatar assured Dieter and Deutsch when he was called to Nahari's office to report on the state of the preparations.

"Very good." said Nahari, obviously pleased "Is there any definite target settlement for the attack?"

"We believe the target will be Moshav Ya'ara, Nahari. We received confirmation of this from our interception of their communications. There was only one thing..."

"What was that, exactly?" Gideon broke in.

"Noam wanted us to incorporate a short fake order from the commander of the military arm, congratulating the Hezbollah force and ordering it to continue the progress. Noam said this would enable us at a later stage to use deepfake technology and disrupt the actual attack on Ya'ara. But we haven't yet decided whether to hold off on activating the tool for a much larger action, and not reveal it too early in the operation."

"Now comes the real test of the defense of Ya'ara!" exclaimed Nahari.

"We need to inform the IDF General Staff and the Northern Command of the latest information we heard on the network. Continue tracking the stages of their operation based on our observation of the exercises they carried out. We know where the opening of the attack tunnel is that will lead to Moshav Ya'ara, but keep in mind that all the settlements on the northern border are potential targets. Every minute could be decisive."

Chapter 13

BEIRUT AND TEL AVIV

"Good morning to you!" said Nasrallah as he entered the "war room" of the military arm. "What progress have you made with our strike force? Is everything going as planned?" he asked the commander of the military branch.

"Yes, Honorable Secretary General, the force is on its way to the entrance of the tunnel that has been well hidden until now. We expect that at any moment they will enter the tunnel."

"What is happening with the enemy? What is the level of alert of the Israeli settlements along the border?"

"All the border settlements have received a warning and their people have entered the bomb shelters. We started an artillery barrage of long-range precision missiles and have had some good results. However," the wing commander added, "many of the missiles were intercepted by the Iron Dome defense system."

"Continue exactly as in the exercises," the commander ordered. "The tunnel is open and secure. It is all now in your hands. Good luck!"

Tense silence reigned in Nahari's operations room where the surveillance was being conducted. The liaison officer of the Northern Command reported heavy shelling from rockets and missiles from Hezbollah artillery on the northern border settlements. Already in the first few minutes, the officer said, he received a report of casualties in three localities. The number of dead and wounded is still unclear. The operational division at the northern border was busy treating the casualties.

"Fortunately," the officer noted, "The Iron Dome was able to intercept a significant number of enemy missiles. In addition, a pre-emptive strike by the Air Force along with swarms of drones managed to hit several Hezbollah launchers before they could launch their missiles."

"As we saw in the preparation exercises, this must be an attack on a settlement by the force going through the tunnel!" exclaimed Gideon. "Are you tracking this?" He turned to Evyatar, "What are you picking up from the 'wasp' broadcasts? And what is Hezbollah's attacking force saying?"

"A large swarm of 'Wasp' drones are synchronized with our air force, marking the locations of the missile launchers, Gideon," Evyatar assured him, "It's working well. A large number of launchers have been neutralized, and many missiles were destroyed before they could be sent. We are following the movement of the Hezbollah ground force and we saw them enter the attack tunnel. They are still inside the tunnel, but we will probably not have radio contact until they get close to its exit."

"Do you know where they are headed?" Dieter asked, "The launch of the missiles was expected in preparation for the ground action."

"We have to wait and see if they attack more than one settlement, even if they allocate the bulk of their force on the particular settlement they have chosen. Evyatar, are we certain that it is Moshav Ya'ara they intend to attack?"

"Dieter is asking good questions, Evyatar. We need the details," Gideon added. "Knowing their precise target, we can concentrate our efforts and optimally carry out the thwarting of the operation."

"There is only one settlement that they are going after and that is Moshav Ya'ara, but several Hezbollah units have received orders to cut through into our territory in several locations in order to confuse us. The attacking force is divided into five units and they intend to take over five or more houses within the moshav."

"A squad from the Golani Brigade is moving towards Ya'ara," the Northern Command liaison officer said. "They are preparing to base themselves in the Taggart fort that has been empty for the past several years. It is in the center of the moshav. Ya'ara's emergency team is patrolling the area to make sure the residents stay in protected areas."

***

"We have exited the tunnel and are advancing," boomed the voice of the Hezbollah operation commander over the loudspeaker. Deafening silence enveloped the operations room of the military arm as everyone held their breath, "Two teams are on their way. Each one is going to take over two houses. There is no one seen outside on the moshav for now. I am on my way to the police building..."

"Continue and may you succeed with the help of Allah, "the military commander urged him.

A sudden staccato burst of gunfire cut off the words of the commander...

***

"The Wasp squadron has discovered the Hezbollah forces!" Noam exclaimed. "They split up into three groups..."

"Golani reports that it has reached the police building," announced the Northern Command liaison officer. "There is no one there and they are preparing for the possibility that Hezbollah forces will arrive..."

Shots are heard in the background...

"What do the 'Wasps' see, Noam?" Dan asked.

"Is it an encounter with the Hezbollah force?"

"Yes, Dan, our standby units opened fire from a distance on a Hezbollah force that tried to enter one of the houses..."

***

"What's going on at the moshav? Who is shooting there? Where did the strike force commander disappear?" shouted Nasrallah.

"There is a battle going on, sir, and we should not interfere in the meantime," Madani replied in an attempt to calm him down. "All forces to the police building now!" came an order from the commander of the military arm to the assault force.

"As ordered, sir," came the voice of the commander of the attacking force.

"Who gave that order in my name?" The commander of the military arm demanded, but none of his men responded. "This could be an enemy trick," replied Madani, "Repeat your order to continue the attack on the Moshav houses."

***

"Something is happening to their communication network!" Noam exclaimed, "There is confusion between the armed command and the Hezbollah attack force at Moshav Ya'ara."

"A Golani unit is engaging the Hezbollah forces," announced the Northern Command liaison officer. "They report that the Hezbollah force has dead and wounded... and Golani also have two wounded fighters..."

***

"Can you tell me what's happening in Ya'ara?" Nasrallah demanded of the commander of the military branch, "Who gave that false order to stop the attack on the Moshav houses and move to the police building?"

"We will find out as soon as possible, Your Honor, but at this stage we need to see to the rescue of our fighters who were not injured in the battle at the police station."

"I believe, Honorable Secretary General," Madani noted sadly, "the enemy successfully used Artificial Intelligence and created confusion in our forces. The military commander is right. It is urgent that we evacuate the rest of our fighters. We will carry out further investigation into the matter later."

While the battle in Moshav Ya'ara continued, the commander of Hezbollah's military arm received a message in the situation room: "All is well. Proceeding according to plan."

It was too late before the hackers from North Korea discovered that this was a fake AI message. Belatedly, Madani informed Hezbollah headquarters in Beirut of this fact.

**

The Mossad's surveillance room resonated with a loud sigh of relief and there were handshakes all around. Evyatar, who had remained at the surveillance screens every moment, explained the confusion created for Hezbollah and Iran. Heads would fall in Lebanon and perhaps also in Iran following the failure of the operation. Evyatar congratulated Noam and Eric for their success in the use of AI. Gideon and Dieter, who had continually followed the action, joined in the congratulations. Gideon reminded Nahari of Dieter's role in the discovery at the last minute of the attack tunnel prepared by Hezbollah.

***

Meanwhile, Nasrallah went on the air and announced a 'victory' for Hezbollah over the Zionist enemy. In Israel and the United States, and even in Tehran, they knew that this false.

***

"Thank you, lady and gentlemen," concluded Nahari, "and please remember that it is our duty, right now, to summarize what we learned from this event, to further understand Hezbollah's moves and come up with strategies for future operations."

Chapter 14

TEHRAN

Madani was unable to sleep. He was awake both during the flight and after landing at the airport in Iran. The failure of Hezbollah fighters in taking over Moshav Ya'ara after the infiltration through the tunnel gnawed at him relentlessly. He knew that General Kashani and the entire Quds Force were waiting.

***

Madani anticipated a tense meeting. Explanations would not be easy. As he entered the meeting room, Kashani's expression left no room for doubt.

"You also think we are humiliated after such a resounding failure, yes? Even though the operatives who failed were 'only' Hezbollah fighters and not our own fighters?"

"Indeed, commander, I cannot sleep because of it. I have examined one by one the points that caused the operation to fail. You stated correctly, General Kashani, that it was essentially an operation by the military force of Hezbollah..."

"We have time before we meet with the leader. Let us hear what points you have come up with. What are the important conclusions for us to present at the meeting with the leader? It is also worth adding concrete recommendations regarding policy improvements, weapons development, and systems that rely on Artificial Intelligence."

"Yes, Commander, this is exactly the direction I am taking in my report. I am ready to speak in detail to the supreme leader as required..."

"Yes? Well, I am listening, Madani."

Madani began: "The artillery barrage on the northern Israeli settlements was not effective enough mainly because of the missile defense systems developed by the enemy. They blocked our communications many times during the operation. We thought the tunnel was undetectable and we were wrong. If we want to continue to operate attack tunnels, we urgently need to make them impossible to detect. The Hezbollah fighters did not operate the intelligence and attack drones that we provided them recently. The enemy, on the other hand, made extensive use of their small spy drones, what they call "Wasps," and their attack drones were also effective. Finally, there was the surprise use by the enemy of deepfake technology to broadcast a false order to the Hezbollah forces. We know about the effectiveness of this tool thanks to information from the Russians, whom we must thank with all our hearts. The concentration of all of Hezbollah's attack forces at the abandoned police building and the bloodbath the enemy was able to unleash on them was due to the fake order, and it was the main reason for the failure of the entire operation."

"You have put together ideas and recommendations that will serve us, I hope, in the future. We must reassure the leader to ensure his continued support, especially in the face of the failure and the issues you will raise. I will ask the leader this morning to allow you to give your summary of the failed operation and your recommendations for the future, which are no less important."

***

Madani, along with General Kashani, commander of the Quds Force, entered the meeting room to report to the supreme leader. To their surprise, the entire top echelon of the Revolutionary Guards was also present. Kashani knew that the severest criticism and rebuke would come from them. The president was seated beside the leader and Kashani knew he would have his support as well as that of the Foreign Minister.

Kashani asked the leader to listen to Madani's impression of the preparations Hezbollah made for the mega-operation as they called it. He recommended that in addition to this, Madani must present an analysis of the operation with emphasis on the reasons for the failure.

"We shall listen to you, my young friend, to understand what happened and what went wrong with Hezbollah's action," encouraged the leader. "Do not hesitate to speak your truth even if it is difficult to understand."

"Thank you very much, Your Honor," Madani began a little apprehensively. "The operation initiated by the commander of Hezbollah's military branch focused on capturing an Israeli settlement in northern Israel and taking all the residents hostage. To prepare for it, they performed exercises with a mock attack tunnel and a proxy for the Israeli settlement," Madani continued, "Unfortunately, this was not sufficient against the technological advantage of the Israeli enemy."

"I cannot understand, honorable leader," the commander of the Revolutionary Guards intervened sharply, "What was our contribution to this important operation? Did the Quds Force choose not to influence the poor planning and failed execution? What was Hezbollah's goal? Merely to raise the morale of the Lebanese?"

"If I may," General Kashani cut in, "I would like to emphasize that the support for this complex operation was carried out according to the policy established by the esteemed leader. Lebanon is in the midst of an economic and social crisis, and it is incumbent on all of us to come to their aid. It is therefore important that we allow Doctor Madani to summarize for us all the stages of the Hezbollah operation. We cannot jump to conclusions that are not sufficiently well-founded."

"Please continue, Doctor Madani, and enlighten us on what happened," the leader reassured Madani, making it clear to the gathering that he was backing him. None of the participants had a word to say after the supreme leader demonstrated his support for the Quds

Force and especially for Madani. His careful preparation and succinct presentation proved to be well accepted, and Madani's confidence grew as he proceeded with his review. He ended his review almost verbatim to the one he had delivered previously to Kashani, by noting that Russia had just agreed to provide deepfake technology to Iran. At the same time, he emphasized that Russia's decision was made only now after the enemy had used an AI deepfake to gain a significant advantage and thwart the operation.

"It seems to me, Your Honor, that we have been given an excellent review from Doctor Madani and he deserves our gratitude," General Kashani addressed the leader. "The Commander of the Revolutionary Guards was right," Kashani added, "in drawing attention to the objectives of the Hezbollah operation. In my opinion, we should view their activities only from the Lebanese perspective on the situation there. We do not need to see the Hezbollah operation as anything more than an attempt to ease Lebanon's crisis and Nasrallah's ambition to be their savior."

"I agree with General Kashani and respectfully suggest, honorable leader, that we adjust our line of action accordingly in the future," added the Iranian president. "Our contribution to Hezbollah's operation in Lebanon, led by Doctor Madani and Quds Force personnel, is worthy of praise. We have heard Madani's review and the gist of the lessons learned from the operation itself, but these are technological by nature, and are important in the broad scope of our strategy. The missiles, the drones, the communications, the prevention of detection of the tunnels; and above all, the recognition of the importance of Artificial Intelligence in our just struggle must be regarded as crucial, as we heard from Doctor Madani."

"We would do well to further strengthen our strategic-military relationship and political support from Russia. I wish to emphasize," continued the minister, "that with all due respect for the advanced weapons, our struggle must have an additional focus: engaging as quickly as possible in the war of the future with Artificial Intelligence. We must master all its applications and use cyber technology for defense and attack capabilities."

"We have heard important information that deserves attention for the improvement of our capabilities. We thank the Quds Force and commander Kashani, and our thanks to Doctor Madani," the leader concluded. "Our decisions must be focused on a major response to the serious damage to our nation from the assassination of General Soleimani, the former commander of the Quds Force and the professor director of all our nuclear development. I thus order the Quds Force to complete the planning of a major revenge operation. May Allah be with you!"

Chapter 15

PALO ALTO

Noam and Eric were due to present the draft of the toolbox to Gideon, who had come especially to Palo Alto, as well as to Dr. Gerald Deutsch and Dan Avni. The draft outlined new technologies gained from their research in the protected SRI laboratory. Eric had proposed that Noam carry out deepfake exercises in the lab to assure their mastery of the technologies. They both had been working since early morning and were eagerly anticipating the visit of Gideon, Deutsch, and Dan. Their long days of toil dealing with Artificial Intelligence and its derivatives were about to be put to the test. Noam was confident that Eric would competently present their findings in computer vision and in the fascinating field of deep-faking. She was also self-assured in the knowledge she had gained in facial expression research and its link to computer vision that she and Eric had discovered, especially the algorithms that direct the production of deepfake.

When everyone was assembled, Eric began: "We are making rapid progress in deepfake technology and we hope to show you its operational capabilities quite soon. We delved deeply into the study of the derivatives of Artificial Intelligence and achieved good control of computer vision..."

"Wait a moment, Eric, you have to start with the basics of computer vision before we can fully understand how it can be used," interjected Dan.

"Don't rush, Eric." Gideon intervened, "Take all the time you need to get us into the thick of computer vision."

"He's a wizard when it comes to derivatives of Artificial Intelligence," Noam said, turning towards Eric, "I suggest you present the review the way you presented it to me, of course shortening it and adapting it for their advanced level of technological knowledge."

Eric smiled and began. "Computer vision is a major research branch of computer science. As a scientific discipline, computer vision deals with the extraction of information from images by automated means. It usually refers to combining automatic image analysis with other means and technologies for automated inspection and process, or robotic guidance in industrial applications. In most practical applications in computer vision, computers are pre-programmed to solve a specific task. The image data can take many forms, such as video sequences, displays from multiple cameras, or multidimensional data" Eric paused momentarily and examined their comprehension level and interest in his explanation thus far.

"The human eye functions as a sort of color video camera with high resolution. The information received is processed and analyzed at lightning speed, sifting the essential from the less essential and deciphering the image with human intelligence. The way this works is still not completely clear to us. Neuroscience and vision researchers have succeeded in partially decoding the process of vision analysis in animals and humans once the beginning of processing and compression of information has occurred in the different layers of the retina, and in various centers in the brain's posterior cortex."

"That's important to know in order to get to the correct processing of the data," Gideon commented. "What more do we know about that, Eric?"

"Researchers are working on ways to imitate the analysis and data processing performed by the human brain when it perceives images. The research is still in its infancy and it will take many more years before we understand the complexity of the human vision system and can imitate it with computerized means."

"You should say a few words about the mechanization aspect of the process," commented Noam. "This is a key point, in my opinion."

"The advantage of mechanization is clear. The quantity of information that cameras can receive, process and analyze is infinitely more accurate and quantitative than the human eye and brain are capable of. Fingerprint recognition software, for example, can scan a database of millions of fingerprints in a brief time to find a match."

"How is this connected to your research into Artificial Intelligence itself? Can you enlighten us on that?" Deutsch asked as he turned to Noam.

"We pretty quickly recognized the interrelation of computer vision and the field of facial vision with analysis of facial expressions. Dan produced for us software that creates visual fakes. That helped us integrate deepfake voice into computer vision software. The voice is based on an audio sample of the character being controlled. It's starting to look like this will be a valuable component of the deepfake toolbox we're building."

"I'm pleased to hear about these applications," Gideon exclaimed, "and hearing about what steps you've taken to implement them."

"Dan found us an algorithm developed at a Canadian university that allows artificial recording based on a voice sample of only a few dozen seconds," Eric noted, "And we integrated it into our algorithm file. It helped in the deepfake exercises we carried out. In the initial exercises, we used Dan's algorithm with our own voices as samples," Noam explained, while fingering the keyboard to demonstrate the surprisingly accurate activation of AI-produced voices. "What we have here," continued Noam, "is an improved version that we achieved after many attempts..."

"It's very convincing." said Dan, obviously impressed, "You really can control the technology. What's next? Where do you go from here?"

"A while ago we found an algorithm developed in the United States that converts written text into sound with the voice of a chosen character. Noam and I were enthusiastic about this technology and we identified several possibilities for quick and convenient use," said Eric. "We still have a lot of work to do on it until the algorithm also becomes integrated into our deepfake toolbox."

"You undoubtedly are aware of the concern in the United States." Noam said to Deutsch, "Your head of national intelligence was asked to assess the threat that deepfakes pose to national security. We read about the real fear that this technology will lead to disinformation and extortion."

"Yes, I know about the concerns in our administration," confirmed Deutsch, "and they are clearly justified. They are leading us to push for new research and development of systems to detect enemy deepfakes, especially by the Iranians and their cohorts in North Korea."

"There is an alarming finding from Evyatar's team that shows that Iran, with the help of hackers from North Korea, is very active in the field of deepfake and already is working on control of AI-generated characters," Dan interjected, "Fortunately, it is still in the beginning stages according to Evyatar, and it is not hard to identify deepfake from Iran at this point. I asked Evyatar to provide you with all the material he's accumulated so far."

"I can also tell you," Eric continued, "that my latest research shows exactly what Evyatar and his people discovered. Iran and North Korea definitely have the capacity to develop these new technologies. We'll be glad if we could get those materials from Evyatar. Noam and I have divided our workload, where Noam focuses on identification and protection technologies and I deal with the attack technologies."

"That sounds like the right move, my young friends," said Deutsch.

"I intend to add to your materials an algorithm developed at the University of Southern California for the detection of counterfeits, as well as innovative algorithms dealing with a variety of automatic counterfeit detection technologies originally developed at the Pentagon's Research Institute of Future Technologies – DARPA." said Noam.

***

"We haven't answered in detail what the next step would be," Noam reminded them, "which is the controlling of the technology and the collection of algorithms in the field of Artificial Intelligence, as well as computer vision and deepfake from the basic framework. We now need to create a pool of key personnel that we will need in both the attack and defense fields. Evyatar and his people can help a great deal in gathering this information, but I am sure, Deutsch, that the intelligence system in the States as well as the databases that exist at DARPA will provide us with a tremendous amount of data, without which it will be extremely difficult for us to carry out our mission successfully."

"You've convinced us of how important and urgent it is to complete your deepfake toolbox," exclaimed Gideon, as Deutsch and Dan nodded their heads in agreement.

"Deutsch is absolutely right," Dan rejoined, "It's important we update Nahari and get Evyatar and his team on this right away to help set up the database of characters."

"Exactly what needs to be done," confirmed Noam, "but Eric came up with the idea of 'reviving' Dieter in his former identity when he was working on behalf of Hezbollah and as a lead scientist for the Iranian Quds Force. Hezbollah and Iran's confusion and frustration in response to the deepfake will confirm that we were successful in completing its development."

Chapter 16

TEL AVIV

Evyatar led the important brainstorming session with his team, along with the participation of the "branch" in California: Dan, Noam, and Eric. The different time zones between Israel and the west coast of the United States meant that they would have to stay awake at highly unusual hours. As a result, the teams on both sides of the globe developed new protection for the communication and transmission of classified data – a system that replaced civilian software systems, such as Zoom or Google Meet. Most importantly, the system was accessible only by the two teams. At the same time, it was impossible to transfer much of Noam and Eric's sensitive technological findings from their research at SRI. The issue of unifying the teams became more urgent as information on the progress of the Iranian threat emerged. Each team had better knowledge in a different specific area, and they complemented each other. In California, the technological part of the algorithms that emerged in Artificial Intelligence and the control of computer vision was developed, as well as entry into the field of deepfake. Conversely, Evyatar's team in Israel controlled the media networks through which the information was streamed. The information left no doubt as to the threats taking shape in Iran. Everyone was of the opinion that a concentrated, integrated effort was essential if they were to cope with the imminent threat.

***

"I will inform Nahari and Gideon of the new threats we identified in the last twenty-four hours." Evyatar had told the researchers in his team.

Meantime, there was tense silence in the team's control room and listening center. In the room were the two graveyard shift team members who hadn't slept a wink. They were now joined by the rest of their colleagues arriving for another day's work, listening and analyzing the findings...

Everyone anxiously awaited Evyatar's return from his meeting at Nahari's office.

***

"Good news!" Evyatar exclaimed on his entry into the control room, back from the meeting. "The head of Mossad received our assessments of the threat from Iran, and on Gideon's advice, our partners from California will be joining us here. Dan, Deutsch, Noam, and Eric are already on their way. In particular, the Mossad was concerned about Iran's anticipated use of the algorithms of the new technology for deepfake, which as we all know, originates from AI."

***

The day the California team landed in Israel, Nahari hurriedly arranged a welcoming committee. Meanwhile, Dan, Noam and Eric had time for a quick trip to Evyatar's "Kingdom." There they were given a briefing; short but interesting and impressive. The review included the new threat recently discovered by Evyatar's team – their use of an encrypted version of Zoom software. It was clear that this had to be developed by a country with advanced high-tech capabilities, probably North Korea, and had been transferred to the Iranians. Evyatar acknowledged that they had not yet unlocked all the details of the encrypted software, but that they soon would. Dan praised the team's achievements and promised to free up time as soon as possible to become more involved after his meeting with Nahari.

Noam, Eric, and Deutsch, accompanied by a cyber-scientist from the U.S. Embassy in Tel Aviv, arrived at the meeting with Evyatar's team. Noam came up with an idea to combine the cracking of the encrypted communications used by the Iranians with the deepfake technology that she and Eric had mastered.

"I don't understand, Noam, what is our goal in the combination you suggest?" asked Evyatar, "Because of the Coronavirus pandemic, Zoom has seen astronomical growth in usage. We know of the recent trend of encryption on Zoom traffic, which is a logical move.

Still, what does the encryption of Zoom software have to do with deepfake? It isn't clear to me."

"An appropriate question, Evyatar. I suggest we hear from Eric about this. He is the most knowledgeable in this area."

"Recently, publications in several countries are focusing on cyber protection guidelines when dealing with video communication on the network," began Eric. "This is partly due to the Coronavirus pandemic. Emergency regulations of various world organizations raised the need for functional intercommunication between diverse entities. This is achieved by using technological infrastructures and applications that allow continued work remotely, away from the office. This increased exponentially during Corona. The basic premise for security is that the information does not exceed a certain low level of confidentiality…"

"I understand what you are saying," Dan interjected, "that Zoom participants are not allowed to transmit confidential information. What about encryption? After all, it can enable transmission at the highest security levels, can't it?"

"That's right, Dan. I'll get to that," Eric replied. "The use of communication video software significantly increases the potential size of the attack surface due to the organization connecting and sharing information in infrastructures over which it has no control. As to efficiency and collaboration at work, using the aforementioned application without implementation of adequate cyber protection will expose the organization's infrastructure and users to a substantial risk of damage to the confidentiality, reliability, and availability of information. By implementing some controls..."

"Eric, you should say a few words about encryption and its importance that you learned about in your research," Noam intervened.

"Right, Noam. It is imperative to use the latest software version and update security regularly. In all cooperative configurations, information encryption mechanisms will be used. An invitation to a video meeting will be made using a secure mechanism, and with positive identification only. Joining without a password is prohibited. At the end of a conversation, all participants need to completely disconnect. The call/video recording option has to be blocked, as well as the information saving option. Capability for securely saving logs and generating reports that are meaningful must be activated. Another crucial element is to call for a periodic review of the list of users of the system. Connecting the organization's switchboard to the service is prohibited," continued Eric.

A lively discussion began. It was clear that this was a new tool for defensive and offensive use. Deutsch, in his assumed role as 'responsible adult,' welcomed the achievements and urged that an update to Gideon and Nahari should be made as soon as possible to share the new ideas and information with them.

Chapter 17

TEHRAN AND MOSCOW

Dr. Madani entered the general's room and sat down opposite him. Despite the long road he had traversed, from research assistant to commander of the Quds Force, he was still tense and nervous whenever he was called to a meeting with General Kashani.

"We are in an uncomfortable situation, Madani." the general began. "Top administration officials, and especially our supreme leader, are concerned about what they call 'a disturbing delay' in revenge. The failures that resulted from incomplete protection of our technological projects, especially the uranium enrichment plants in Natanz, are also subject to sharp criticism. I am sure, Madani, that there is no need to tell you that the threat from the generals in the Revolutionary Guard is ongoing; they are just waiting for us to make a mistake..."

"I understand that, Commander. I have no doubts about the seriousness of the internal threat you mention. We will not be able to justify the delay only by the failure of the intelligence systems or our somewhat lax treatment of the cyber threat to our communications system. Recently, as you know, we have strengthened the department responsible for developing Artificial Intelligence technologies. That does not solve all the problems, but it is encouraging progress."

"That is so, but it does not eliminate the accusations against you personally for having 'opened a travel agency' so to speak... Our opponents in the Revolutionary Guards do not rest for a moment and feed the supreme leader with slander, some of which, unfortunately, is justified. What do you propose to do now?"

"I have set up a meeting today," Madani hastened to reply, "with the new director of the development of strategic systems, including and especially, in the development of nuclear weapons. This is a follow-up meeting after the discussion in your office a few days ago. He controls a large number of scientists and is not beholden to the Revolutionary Guard. I intend to ask for his help, together with the scientists under him. I believe it will be a major contribution to the issues we are dealing with... There is something else. I'm talking about a recently developed air-to-ground cruise missile, the Kh-47M2, called the 'Kinzhal.' It is a Russian nuclear-capable hypervelocity aero-ballistic air-to-surface missile. The missile can be launched from the new MiG-31 and Sukhoi Su-57 aircraft and it travels at ten times the speed of sound. The missile can hit targets more than two thousand kilometers distant..."

"What was it designed to do?"

"To target US and NATO warships that pose a threat

to Russia's strategic missile systems. The Kinzhal can neutralize the NATO missile defense system and destroy ships that provide defense against ballistic missiles. It is purportedly able to overcome all known or future-planned air defense systems of the United States, including the American Patriot and THAAD missiles and even the Israeli Arrow missiles."

"But will the Russians be willing to give us use of this great missile?"

"If they do, we will have the capacity to take revenge on the United States and on Israel in a most significant way."

"Good. Try to obtain them. Don't waste time on anything that won't advance our cause. Remember you have the support of the supreme leader for you and your team's visit to

Russia."

***

Madani met with the new director of nuclear weapons development, the successor of murdered Professor Mohsen Fakhrizadeh. He told the new director about his intention to avenge the martyred scientist – may God bless his soul – and about his recent visit to North Korea.

"I had substantive meetings with General Lee," Madani informed him, "and I felt that the strategic relationship between us and North Korea was solid and even strengthened."

"Indeed. I also met General Lee on a previous-trip to Pyongyang and found him to be an unusual combination of a daring warrior and a brilliant research and development scientist," said the new director of nuclear development.

"I have no doubt that I will also have a good relationship with the general."

"I asked for this meeting with you, Professor," continued Madani, "to analyze and evaluate the state of development of our nuclear weapons, especially now that the chief nuclear scientist is no longer with us. I would like to hear from your honor what country we can turn to for support in nuclear technology. North Korea? China? Or maybe Russia after all?"

"North Korea," the professor replied, "is the most worthwhile candidate for partnership and support in the transfer of nuclear weapons technologies. It has withdrawn from the NPT, the non-proliferation treaty, and does not take into account the rules of supervision of the IAEA, which is based in Vienna. North Korea is therefore free, unlike the other nuclear powers, to provide us with information and material assistance for the development of nuclear weapons."

"And who else can we approach? Russia? Or maybe China, which over the years has been a loyal supporter of North Korea?" Madani pressed further.

"To the best of my knowledge, Doctor Madani, my friend," the professor replied, "Russia has not given nuclear secrets to any country, except for the ones that were in the former Soviet Union. And its compliance with the six-power agreement with Iran regarding the restriction of nuclear weapon development is not an encouraging indication. Perhaps," the professor pondered aloud, "there is a possibility to appeal 'only' to individual scientists who were made redundant as researchers in the field of nuclear physics. There is a considerable number of Russian scientists who might agree to aid us, of course with the Moscow government turning a blind eye."

"I would like to raise another strategic issue related to Russia, professor. I am referring to the supersonic cruise missiles Russia has developed. If the Russians agree to share with us the secret of this technology, we can develop a suitable means for the 'Great Revenge' the supreme leader has ordered us to carry out. Do you think this is a good idea? Is it possible?" The professor did not answer immediately and Madani began to fear he would dismiss the idea altogether.

"Yes, Doctor Madani, that is actually a worthy idea and even more likely than the Russians sharing nuclear information with us. You must speak to them about this. Sometimes there is agreement at the top level and it takes a long time for it to filter down. Indeed, your upcoming visit to Russia will be an excellent opportunity to see how we can promote the issue of supersonic cruise missiles."

Madani left the meeting feeling reassured. At the end of it, the professor had agreed to join him on the Russian visit. The relationship between the research systems of the two countries, the professor had noted, allowed him to participate in scientific conferences held in Moscow and he was certain such meetings would serve as a good place to discuss the missiles.

Business class on the Russian airline Aeroflot was ornate and luxurious. Already when they arrived at the Aeroflot lounge at Tehran International airport, Madani felt that something good was in the making. The Russians' treatment of the professor, Madani, and the young scientist from Madani's team who accompanied them on the visit as an escort, was excellent. The professor commented that there are no accidents in Russia and that the special treatment probably came directly from President Putin's office.

"Most of the visit, in my opinion, will not deal with military issues, but with the nuclear electric power plants, such as our reactors at the Bushehr site, and they will certainly not pass up an opportunity to give us a detailed description of dealing with the Chernobyl disaster."

"Indeed, I agree that is what will happen, professor, but let's not forget the issue of the cruise missiles. I broached the subject on my previous meeting with President Putin."

***

"Welcome to Moscow!" They were welcomed by a colonel in uniform with an impressive row of medals emblazoned on his chest. "I am happy to meet you. I will be at your disposal and do all I can for the success of your visit."

Madani whispered into the professor's ear that he was sure the escort was a senior officer of Russian intelligence with a dual mission of helping coordinate the visits and meetings, while at the same time providing intelligence oversight for the Russian security services.

"Thank you, Colonel. We look forward to the meetings and visits to the research institutions that you have prepared for us," Madani praised him while flipping through the visitation folder the colonel handed him. An identical copy was given to the professor.

"I see that you have arranged a meeting with the minister of defense for us. Quite an honor."

"Yes, Doctor Madani. Defense Minister General Sergey Korchenko asked to meet you and his request was sanctioned by President Putin. The minister intends to clarify our relationship with you and with Syria, which receives military and political support from us. Following the information received during the preparations for your visit," the colonel continued, "the defense minister is troubled by the intervention of the Israeli army and especially its air force. The continuous attacks are detrimental to your activities and ours in supporting President Assad's government."

These are strategic and political issues," the professor quickly interjected, looking over the titles on the visitation schedule. "We had thought of focusing on the technological field."

"Yes, the professor is correct," Madani commented, adding, "In any case, we will hear what your intentions are and update our leadership on our return to Tehran."

"That is fine," replied the colonel, "Here we are at your hotel. You should have a rest before the marathon of meetings in the coming days."

***

The next three days, as the accompanying officer had forewarned them, were jam-packed with trips to electrical power plants. Top scientists were called upon to update Madani and the professor on the latest developments in the structure of nuclear power plants. Madani listened with interest to what the Russians and Ukrainians had learned from analyses of the Chernobyl disaster. From time to time, the professor whispered technical explanations of the complex details of the summary. Madani was astounded by the descriptions of sacrifice and dedication of those who had been brought in to clean up the epic radioactive breakdown that resulted in the deaths of so many of them. A particularly important aspect of the visit was how to handle the nuclear fuel prior to installation in the core, and storage of the fuel after it had served its purpose. Preparing the fuel rods for Iran's power reactors at the site near Bushehr was outlined in detail. Also the absorption and storage of the irradiated fuel, after it finished its role in the reactor core was presented as the latest word in the technology of power reactors. Madani's questions related to nuclear weapons development, however, were treated politely, but without actual substance.

***

"President Putin has asked to meet with you personally in his office within the hour." Madani was informed by the accompanying officer when the visits to the nuclear facilities were complete. Madani was pleased but concerned about this completely unexpected invitation.

"What might Putin bring up in a meeting with me?" Madani wondered as he turned to the professor. "Perhaps this is an opening to the more strategic issues? Maybe it is concerning the hypersonic cruise missiles?"

"Maybe," replied the professor, "but it is possible that he will raise the issue of aid to Syria and a call for more intensive activity in the face of attacks by the Israeli Air Force."

***

"I am glad to meet you, Doctor Madani," Putin said, shaking Madan's hand with unexpected force. "I want to raise an issue," the president hastened to add. "And you, in your position with the supreme leader, will be able to deliver the message the best way possible."

"Certainly, Mr. President, of course, I will convey it with pleasure."

"This concerns the political and military aid we provide to Syria," Putin began as he waited for his words to be translated. "Recently, we have seen serious involvement not only of Israel, but mainly from the United States in supporting the Syrian rebel organizations. We have the Syrian army and the welcome involvement of Hezbollah fighters, but this is not enough. You must do more to support al-Assad without obliging us to enter into armed conflict with the United States. My request, Doctor Madani, comes with our recognition of your country's indisputable influence in the region," he complimented his guest. "and I'm sure you will know how to raise Iran's level of aid to the Syrian regime."

***

"Without question, your honor, the message will be delivered as soon as possible to the supreme leader."

"You have my trust, Comrade Madani," Putin chose the sobriquet reserved for Russian officials. He added, "Is there another topic you wish to raise?"

"Indeed yes, your honor," Madani continued, seizing on Putin's encouragement and amiability. "We also thought, as part of the deployment of the Quds Force, that it is necessary to directly attack the leaders of the opposing forces in Syria, those who also threaten you... that is...eliminating the head of the CIA and the head of the Mossad. But, Honorable President, we need your help with the advanced weapons we could use to carry out such a plan..."

"You mean the cruise missiles?" Putin was taken aback and was silent for several moments. Madani held his breath and refrained from repeating himself. On one hand, Madani was sure that the idea he proposed was in line with Putin's strategic global view as a former KGB man, but he did not know how far Putin would allow himself to go at this time.

"I do not rule out the idea, Comrade Madani, but a sensitive and complex move such as this requires careful preparation and planning. Do I understand that this issue has not yet been presented for the approval of your supreme leader? We will move forward after I hear from you of such approval. Only then will we form a joint team to recommend how to put together the details of the operation."

"Thank you, Honorable President, for your support," Madani said, "This is the beginning stage of an extraordinary act. I will return and update you after the supreme leader hears of the plan and gives his approval so we can move forward."

Chapter 18

STANFORD

It was the start of a typical day for Dr. Deutsch at Stanford's SRI. As usual, most of the researchers were already perched in front of their computer screens that were switched on non-stop. Deutsch waited, along with his deputy for advanced technologies, for the arrival of Dr. Dieter Grossfeld. The flight from Berlin had just landed at San Francisco International Airport and the institute's marketing director was bringing Grossfeld directly to the institute. Deutsch had postponed his flight to Israel with Dan and Noam, so that he could confer with Grossfeld.

***

"Welcome, Dieter," Deutsch rose from his chair to shake the hand of his guest. "Sorry to say that your son Eric has already left with Dan Avni and his wife Noam on their way back to Israel. But you will see him there when we go on to the next stage of the plan."

"I understand, Dr. Deutsch. I was hoping to see him

here, but I was delayed by activities at the University in Berlin. During my contact with the researchers there, I saw how particular they are and I did not want to leave any issues unresolved. I will see Eric in Israel on the next phase of the research that Dr. Ben Ari has set up. I assume, Dr. Deutsch, that you have heard from Gideon about their intention to have us both serve as the project's overseers at the Mossad."

"Yes, Dieter. We're happy to have you here at the institute. I have assigned two excellent doctoral students to you to assist you in gathering and analyzing material."

"Thank you. I am somewhat familiar with the research program. It seems to be a multifaceted and ambitious one. Gideon told me about it when we met at the Berlin conference. I trust his judgment completely on the chances of success. And he had warm praise for my son Eric who specializes in the complex technology of Artificial Intelligence. I would love to hear more from you, Dr. Deutsch, about his achievements during his post-doctorate year with you."

"Your son amazes us all with his knowledge and serious approach to research. Eric and Noam Avni are a great team, delving deeply into the forefront of AI derivatives," confirmed Deutsch. "Fortunately, they have a terrific coordinator and instructor in Dan Avni, who supervises and completes background research."

"I would like to add something," said the assistant for advanced technologies, "and mention Eric's expertise in deepfake. It's his doing that resulted in an innovative algorithm for the technology. Eric's knowledge is phenomenal, and he helped Dr. Noam Avni, who relied on his work to complete her doctorate in facial expression analysis. Their collaboration gave us new tools for Artificial Intelligence and its derivatives. For both defense and attack."

"There is another innovative field Eric and Noam are working on," added Deutsch, "a field related to online video calls that became so widespread during Corona."

"They keep on innovating?" Dieter marveled. "What now?"

"A new type of security communication similar to Zoom. It's a brand new field, which enables completely secure communication," said Deutsch proudly. "These two young people – your son Eric and Gideon's daughter Noam – are in the thick of things when it comes to secure communication and cracking encrypted communication by others. We recently learned here in Palo Alto, with the help of Mossad research in Israel, that North Korea transferred information about this to Iran."

"I understand, Dr. Deutsch, that the subject you have prepared for my research is not particularly broad. Can we assume the research will advance us in adding to the toolbox you mentioned earlier? Can you give me more details?" Dieter wondered as he directed his question to the assistant in advanced technologies at SRI.

"Yes, Dr. Grossfeld," replied the deputy, "we intend to expand our knowledge in the field of computer vision. I will update you later on what we know so far and what we still need so that we can integrate this technology into the systems we already have in the toolbox in Israel. You'll be glad to know, Dieter, that Eric has already made important progress on computer vision. He passed on information to Noam that will help her integrate the analysis of facial expressions into deepfake technology."

***

The institute's guest apartment, which Eric had previously occupied, was now at his father Dieter's disposal. He took advantage of the break in discussions and caught up on hours of sleep he had missed. The secure laboratory made available to Noam and Eric contained everything he needed for further research on computer vision. After a few days, in which the deputy for technologies catered to Dieter's every request, he felt that he had accumulated enough material to report on his findings.

Deutsch was in constant contact with Dieter every day and appreciated the pace of the research progress. He updated Dieter on the schedule for the flight to Israel and his linking up with the team there. Deutsch told him the staff were looking forward to his arrival and were very happy he would be joining them.

***

""Hello and welcome my dear friend!" Gideon exclaimed as he hugged Dieter who had come with Deutsch straight from the airport to Nahari's office.

"It's good to see you again. I have much to tell you

and lots of questions. But you had a long flight and first you deserve a rest."

"You're right about that long flight from California. It would be good to take a break and rest. But first, I want to see my son. I heard a lot of praise from Deutsch about his work and I have to confess I am not surprised!"

Dan and Noam accompanied Dieter to the cyber center run by Evyatar and gave father and son a few moments of privacy. Dan said a few words about Eric and Noam's mastering of deepfake technology. He insisted that if it weren't for their joint efforts, they wouldn't be as advanced in the technology as they were. Dan added that after Dieter had some rest, that he, Gideon, and perhaps also Deutsch, would present a comprehensive review and update on all the research and relevant activities thus far.

***

A few hours later, Dieter was up and about.

"Thank you, Gideon, I've had enough rest and I'm ready to catch up," said Dieter. "I hope that my stay in California and the brief research I did at Dr. Deutsch's institute, will help conceal my collaboration with the team here. I believe that my research partners at the University of Berlin are certain I am still at the institute in California. Hats off to Dr. Deutsch's 'cunning strategy.' How do you propose I fit into the team the young people are leading?"

"From this moment on we are both senior advisors to Nahari."

"Great – I am eager to continue my research."

"The short but impressive work you did in the field of computer vision has contributed to the subject and the team of young researchers has already put it to use. It is also part of your concealment scheme. We will receive continual updates on the team's operations as well as the activities of Iran and North Korea. A new, even more threatening front can be added, coming from the Russians. Their strategy in Syria and support for Iran will keep us busy. Nahari expects us, as senior advisors, to provide a different perspective and an independent opinion on the threats and the responses that the team will recommend."

"Happy to serve as advisor with you, Gideon. I am ready to be updated on the status of the activity, both in defense and attack, with the new tools at our disposal. But I recall, Gideon, that we have another issue Eric spoke to me about not long ago."

"Remind me...is it about deepfake?"

"Yes, this should bring our attention back to 'Dr. Nimer al-Khaldi,' whom both the Iranians and Hezbollah have lost track of. You have a great deal of video material with my previous image and also quite a few audio tracks. Eric thought that using them would provide important practice for deepfake technology, but particularly it would confound our enemies and enable us to lead them astray, and ultimately to a dead end. What do you say? Is the technology ready to be utilized?"

"An excellent idea of Eric's. Of course, it will require a very cautious operation. This is where your involvement is very necessary, my friend. Without it there is no point in trying this strategy. Nahari already gave the idea a green light and we can set it into motion after final planning."

"I am ready to be of service to Evyatar and the entire team in bringing 'Nimer' back to life. But surely they are busy with other issues?"

"We have our first operational activity by Evyatar and his men, based on the joint deepfake research of Eric and Noam. It is intended for use against Iran and North Korea and perhaps in the future against Russia as well. I advised Nahari to take time to observe the young people's presentation of the new capability. We heard a recording made by Evyatar. He and his team intervened in a conference call the Hezbollah leader and commander of the Quds Force had with Doctor Madani and were able to alter it. Nahari is convinced that this is an innovative and promising development. I can be a 'silent observer' in the process and would assist only in extreme cases."

Chapter 19

TEHRAN

A special meeting was held in Madani's office. Three senior aides were summoned for a situational assessment and consultation. General Kashani had given over to Madani's care the disturbing complaints from the military wing of Hezbollah and from Syrian intelligence. Kashani had demanded of Madani that the sporadic disruption of communications between Hezbollah and the Syrian Quds Force be rigorously scrutinized. He again stressed that the Revolutionary Guard generals were just waiting for the Quds Force to make mistakes so they could take advantage of them and gain favor with the supreme leader.

Madani himself was also aware of other economic aspects. He knew how important it was for the Quds Force to maintain their payments from the state. Kashani did not think to mention the prestige and privileged status that the Quds Force had, thanks to the many years and successful leadership of the late martyr General Soleimani.

***

"What do you know about the communication failures?" Madani pressed the aides after describing to them General Kashani. "Is the problem with us? Or is it only with our Hezbollah friends in Lebanon, Hamas in the Gaza Strip, and in Syria? What do you say?" Madani turned to the senior of the three aides who served as his deputy.

"I am not certain, Dr. Madani. It is definitely possible that it was a cyber-attack. And if it can happen here, with all the security of our networks, it is clear that in Lebanon, Gaza, and Syria, it is much more likely. We have a reasonably good professional relationship with our colleagues in the Revolutionary Guard, sir, and they don't know much more than we do about the progress which the enemy has attained in cyber-attack technology."

"But the problems are deeper than just the communication breakdown," said Madani, "all our assistance to Syria and Hezbollah in transferring advanced weapons is in danger due to attacks by the Zionist entity's air force on Syrian convoys. How do they know the exact routes of the convoys and their schedules? What has happened to the anti-aircraft defense against the planes and the drones that we developed and made available to the Syrians?"

"Doctor Madani, sir, you are right. The communication failures and the inability to protect the weapons convoys in Syria are interconnected..."

"If you'd allow me, Dr. Madani," the second aide intervened, "it seems to me that the main complaints about Lebanon, Gaza, and Syria stem from an unprotected use of the means we made available to them. This can also be seen in Zoom media. Zoom provides an easily accessible and convenient cyber connection, but it is definitely not secure..."

"So, this is another area, the video calls, where failures abound. Where will it end? Madani complained.

"With your permission, sir," the third assistant aide ventured, "I recently came across several articles, publicly accessible documents to be exact, that mention a new development that guarantees secure audio and video online communication. The articles do reveal cover-ups and subterfuge, but scientists in Moscow, whose knowhow we have already begun to call upon, are most certainly familiar with this issue. Doctor Madani, may I suggest consulting with the Russians as soon as possible in this area."

"Thank you, my friends, we have made some progress in understanding the threat and the direction of efforts to deal with them. I accept the recommendation for face-to-face meetings with the Russian scientists and with their hired hackers in particular. Today, I will ask for the approval of General Kashani for meetings in Moscow and I will recommend that the three of you join me. Please remain where you are for a moment," Madani turned and addressed the aide who had already stood up to leave. "I have not yet brought up another problem that requires attention, especially yours."

Madani began, not taking his eyes off the aide, "I refer to the discovery of Hezbollah's tunnels in the north and those of Hamas on the Gaza border..."

"I remember, Doctor Madani, that the issue of tunnel protection was highly classified. Only Doctor Nimer al-Khaldi knew all the details of the defense systems. Now we know that the responsibility for the whole issue is yours, commander, so what do we need to do? And what is my role?"

"I recommended to General Kashani to put the matter of the defense of the tunnels in your hands, and he approved," replied Madani. "I am too busy with other issues, some of which we have just spoken about," Madani added. "Our responsibilities include contact with Hezbollah and Hamas, but also, and no less important, to promote contact with Russia, which has been a leader in this field since prior to the Second World War. In fact, we know that Russia gave North Korea information about the construction and fortification of tunnels that enabled them to effectively wage war against South Korea, which was supported by the United States and other western countries. During our upcoming visit to Moscow, we will learn about the latest improvements in tunnel defense systems. When we return to Tehran, you can upgrade our systems and we will be able to help Hamas and Hezbollah improve the defense systems for their tunnels. It's no secret that a great deal of effort and investment is required to improve the defense of attack tunnels. They have already yielded good results in the north and south."

"Ah..." stammered the self-conscious assistant, "I did not expect to go into such a sensitive and important subject as this. I believe we have a lot to learn from the Russians in this area. Thank you, commander, for your trust. I will do everything possible to justify it. Do I understand correctly that this is part of what is assigned to us on our next trip to Russia?"

"We are starting a project to assemble hypersonic cruise missiles with the ability to reach targets thousands of kilometers away. We have Russia's agreement in principle, with President Putin's authorization, to make available to us full information on high-speed missile technology, and we have the approval of our supreme leader."

"I cannot believe my ears, Commander. Is this truly happening? Is Russia willing to divulge such advanced technology?"

"Yes, my friend, these missile systems are so fast that enemy missile defense systems are ineffective against them. The Russians will not provide us with the actual missiles, but they will give us the technological knowledge for us to complete their development and equip ourselves with these missiles in a relatively short time."

"Dr. Madani, we need to designate specific targets for such missiles. What is my role in this formidable project?"

"You will oversee the development of the Iranian version of the high-speed missiles with a small, top-secret group of partners. The goal," Madani whispered, "is the integration of these missile systems into our mega revenge operation that the supreme leader has ordered us to prepare. Most importantly we must establish personal contact with the scientific community of the Russian security system. You need to make preparations immediately for our visit."

Only five passengers besides Madani were in the business class lounge at Tehran airport, waiting for an Aeroflot flight to Sheremetyevo International Airport. Madani had included his chief aide, two senior researchers, and two top scientists to deal with the technology for the advanced missiles in their meetings with the Russians. The Aeroflot flight attendants in the lounge made sure to pamper these passengers who had all been upgraded to business class. Madani said that this was undoubtedly a directive from above, most likely an order from Putin himself.

"I hope the Russians understand and accept all our requirements and they prepare meetings accordingly for us," said Madani's chief aide, who was constantly worried. He went on, "Do you think they will reveal cyber war issues, such as telling us in detail how they defend against spyware systems? And not just feed us some crumbs?"

Madani reassured him, "Well, these areas the Russian researchers and hackers are certainly very familiar with. I believe they will help us and expect something from us in return. One word from Putin can really open the door wide for us."

"We have heard about the encryption for online video calls," the technology researcher said, "and we have already received requests for this knowhow from Hezbollah in Lebanon, Hamas in Gaza, and from Syria. They wish to integrate encryption into their communication systems. I hope the Russians allow their cyber experts to extend their encryption capability to us as well."

"There are two additional topics we want to discuss with the Russians," Madani moved on to other issues. "Do you remember we asked them to include in our talks the issue of the small drones developed by Israel that cause us so much damage? The Zionist enemy calls them 'wasps.' So far, we have not heard about the Russians developing similar systems. But we have to assume that they have, and are keeping them secret for future surprise attacks."

"And what is the second issue, Doctor Madani?" asked one of the senior nuclear scientists. "Maybe it has to do with the nuclear issues they have not yet disclosed too much information about?"

"Indeed, that was exactly what I was going to say," Madani hastened to answer. "Putin has not authorized Russian nuclear scientists to share this sensitive data with us. On our previous visit, when the director of nuclear research was still with us, we received a great deal of information on nuclear power plants, including confidential details about the disaster at Chernobyl. I will try in my meeting with Putin to set the security bar a little higher. Perhaps he will agree to turn a blind eye and allow us to employ nuclear scientists who have been made redundant. Most of them would not join us without approval from above."

"Yes, Doctor Madani, that is what we were thinking back in the days when the technological leader we all adored was with us, may Allah avenge his blood."

"That will be on our agenda, completing the list of

topics for our meetings. For your ears only, I intend to bring up the supersonic cruise missiles in the conversation with Putin," Madani concluded. He told his men to rest and prepare for the visit, which surely would be stimulating and highly important.

***

Madani was expecting the reception they were greeted with on their arrival in Moscow. A senior officer with the rank of colonel, the counter-espionage man who had accompanied them on the previous visit, was there to welcome them. However, the surprise came when the colonel announced that President Putin wished to meet Madani immediately. Putin's limousine was waiting, along with another officer from the FSB, who saluted Madani and escorted him to the vehicle, which then quickly drove them to their destination.

***

Madani was led to the meeting room where Putin and his dreaded handshake awaited him...Madani opened the discussion.

"The flight and the crew were above and beyond all expectations, Mr. President, and we are grateful. I have been asked by our supreme leader to convey a special personal greeting to you. The leader asked once again to thank you for your generous support. He knows how much of what we do is made possible thanks to you."

"I have ordered my people to cooperate with you fully," Putin responded, "and tomorrow you will meet with Minister of Defense, General Korchenko, who will hear your concerns. He is a good and loyal man and I trust him. We have prepared a comprehensive tour of the technological facilities and the missile and space development laboratories for your people. I am sure that during your visit, new issues will arise, including your request for assistance in the development of the supersonic cruise missiles and for further cooperation between us."

"Thank you, Honorable President, for your generosity and support. This will enable us to carry out revenge against the Americans and Israel for the assassination of General Soleimani," stressed Madani before taking leave of the Russian president with another bone-chilling handshake.

***

The next morning, Madani took his routine run on the treadmill in the gym of Moscow's luxurious Hotel Metropol, and arrived full of energy at the hotel dining room. His men were already sitting with plates loaded with fine food from the buffet table. He just had time to join them when the escort officer arrived. He greeted them, stating that they had a busy day of scheduled visits and meetings ahead of them.

***

The Defense Ministry's office in the Kremlin was almost as fancy as President Putin's. The two-person meeting was actually a three-person meeting with the presence of the interpreter from the Institute of Foreign Relations and Languages. Madani felt comfortable from the moment he met Defense Minister General Sergey Korchenko, recognizing that he was clearly Putin's trusted enforcer. The meeting began with mentioning the operations: First, the killing of the commander of the Quds Force, General Soleimani with the help of American attack drones. This was followed by the attack on the professor, the director of the nuclear programs by a remotely activated machine gun and the explosion of the vehicles, which all led finally to an in-depth discussion about drones and the use of AI technology.

***

"We learned how to devise our own drones from studying an American drone shot down over our territory. We discovered how to make them fly at low altitudes to avoid radar detection and also about the drone's encrypted communication with its operators. Sir, I can tell you that we have already developed our own small drones similar to those which the Israelis have been operating for a considerable time..."

"This is an impressive achievement, Doctor Madani. For some reason we have not dealt with this issue ourselves." General Korchenko admitted with a frankness that surprised Madani.

"Perhaps we will make this issue our first for technological cooperation?" Madani offered. "We would be happy to transfer to your people the entire research and development portfolio that enabled us to complete the project,"

"That would be a welcome proposal, doctor, and of course President Putin has ordered the immediate appointment of a team of experts in missile technology who will soon arrive in Tehran and assist your people in the development of your version of the missiles."

As the meeting progressed, Defense Minister Korchenko informed Madani what else his people would learn from the meetings with the Russian scientists.

"The young Iranians," said the general, "are amazed by the innovations presented by scientists of the Russian defense system, and especially by those built on derivatives of Artificial Intelligence. Machine learning and data mining," continued the general, "already form an important part of the response arsenal that our researchers have developed.

"But I saw that you also wanted to discuss nuclear issues. Is this still on the agenda?" The Defense Minister surprised Madani.

"It remains our biggest problem, General. It became clear to us during our previous visit to you, that sadly we will not receive direct technological help from Russia in the field of nuclear weapons. It remains for us, perhaps, to examine the recruitment of former nuclear scientists who are currently not working in the field. What do you say to that?" The defense minister was silent for what seemed to Madani to be an exceedingly long time. Madani, meanwhile hesitated to directly raise the issue of North Korean assistance.

General Korchenko finally looked up and said he would consult with the president again on what Russia can divulge to Iran.

"What we might be able to do," Madani tried to continue, "is to host in our country past experts and give them a free hand to continue the research they started. You would surely have no problem not having to finance such a technological laboratory. In this way, you will not be directly involved. What do you think President Putin would say about that?

"I understand, Doctor, the immense importance you attach to this subject. I will discuss it with President Putin and keep you informed."

Later on in the meeting, Madani brought up in detail the unfortunate issue of blockages in the communication systems. He described the distress of running video communications that were obstructed many times. He described the exposure of the tunnels both on the Gaza Strip border and on the Israel-Lebanon border due to the technological systems developed by the enemy. Madani went on to present the general problem of cyber advances in defense and attack, all under the roof of Artificial Intelligence. Not surprisingly, General Korchenko was up to date on this problem and he addressed Madani's concerns with his professional insight. The general noted that he had ordered his men who were hosting the meetings to review the technological status of all the subjects Madani raised in their meeting.

"Your people will also receive an overview on the subject of the tunnels. They will be given details of the composition of the material except, of course, for the secret component that completes the assembly of the defense network, the full formula of which only you will be told."

"I must share with you, General Korchenko, a strange incident we heard about from the commander of the military wing of Hezbollah. We heard about it, but did not believe the 'appearance' of Nimer al-Khaldi in a video call with the Hezbollah commander. As you know, Nimer disappeared a while ago and is probably being held by the Israelis. We wonder, is this a new use of deepfake?"

"We would be interested if Hezbollah would pass on the recording of this conversation to us."

"We received this surprising and disturbing information recently from the Hezbollah commander. He informed Secretary-General Nasrallah, but the matter was kept top secret. You remember the case of the disappearance of Dr. Nimer al-Khaldi and the fear that he was taken to Israel willingly or by force. In the recorded passage in question, Nimer claimed that at the end of the first Lebanon War, Hezbollah did nothing to protect the Palestinian refugees in the Sabra and Shatila camps, where his wife and two of his children were murdered by the Christian Phalangists along with hundreds of other Palestinian refugees. Nimer added another harsh claim about Hezbollah, that while he was working with the Revolutionary Guards in Iran to take revenge on the Israeli enemy, they did not fulfill their obligation to protect his sister and the only son he had left alive. They disappeared from their home in the

Shatila camp. The recorded conversation with the commander was saved and sent to us," said Madani, "After an initial check, our cyber people believe this was an actual conversation and not a deepfake," Madani added.

"You did well, Doctor Madani, to bring this to our attention." General Korchenko said. "Forward the recording to us as soon as possible so that our experts can examine it. This deepfake issue stems from Artificial Intelligence. Our people are knowledgeable about deepfake. It is clear that its use is growing. The situation requires technological monitoring and effort to develop identification and protection on one hand, and also for using this technology for attack purposes, on the other hand."

"Good to know, General, that you are aware of the aggressive falsifications and I hope you can make this important information available to our people."

"Consider it done," promised the general. "We will inform you of our findings as soon as possible."

Madani knew that the general could be taken at his word.

Chapter 20

TEL AVIV

Gideon arrived at the Evyatar team offices for a debriefing on the operation in Iran.

"Congratulations, my young friends!" Gideon began, "Your remarkable cyber-attack disabled the entire Iranian railroad network. Nahari personally told me how pleased he was. I understand you've got a preliminary summary of the operation. Are there any findings that will enable us to damage other strategic targets? Again, you've done an excellent job!"

"Thanks, Gideon, and we appreciate the praise from the head of the Mossad. The operation was a reminder to the Iranians that we can incapacitate parts of their national infrastructure. If we take it one step further, we need to go into additional technological fields based on what we learned from the operation on the railway. We can celebrate our success, but we have to prepare for more new threats."

Evyatar led the team of young people in a discussion on the latest findings regarding Iran's activity in AI technology. Iran's previous relationship had only been with North Korea, but now, with Russia in the picture, things were more dangerous. When a call came from the head of the Mossad praising him for the success of the cyber-attack on Iran's railway system, Evyatar warned that there were concrete threats that had not yet been dealt with.

"What exactly do you define as a 'concrete' threat, Evyatar? An attempt to get at our strategic infrastructure? The development of new technology or a new threat?" Gideon persisted.

"Not necessarily a new threat, but the threats are real and concern our strategic substructure. We're talking about derivatives of AI, a menacing addition to the Iranian toolbox. And Russia's in the game. Putin has decided to give them technological assistance." Evyatar went on. "I suggest you join our upcoming meeting, Gideon, to gauge this new Russian connection. We intend to pay particular attention to the derivatives of Artificial Intelligence they're developing. But even with what already exists, we have had some difficulty with our monitoring of Iranian communications..."

"I thought you had overcome all the obstacles in the covert listening setup," exclaimed Gideon.

"It's happened that we can suddenly lose connection from Syria, Hezbollah in Lebanon, and Hamas in the Gaza Strip. Likewise, there are sporadic disruptions in our viewing of their Zoom meetings, sometimes blocked by cyber defense. And there's another even more disturbing issue," Evyatar continued. "The Iranians have improved their ability to block our own systems. I suggest we inform Deutsch and Nimer and get their help in solving these latest problems. The meeting I am setting up will help clarify the situation. It's worthwhile your being there."

"We will be, Evyatar, I know it's important," replied Gideon, who found Evyatar's recommendations in alignment with his and Nimer's roles as chief advisors. "We will be happy to listen to everything you have to say."

***

"It will be good hearing about these new threats you uncovered," Noam exclaimed when she joined Dan and Eric in a preparatory meeting with Evyatar before the entire team gathered at Nahari's. "I think Gideon and Nimer joining us is important, and maybe even Deutsch will find time to turn up."

"We are dealing with several topics. Each one of them is important and worthy of in-depth investigation," said Dan, who assumed the role of the responsible adult in charge of the young team. "Eric, why don't you begin? Tell us what you have learned about data mining and machine learning."

"Let me start with machine learning. It's a subfield in computer science and AI, the initial activity for statistics and optimization. It deals with the development of algorithms that enable computers to learn from example, and to perform a variety of computational tasks where classical programming is not possible..." Eric paused for a moment and saw that the others were listening intently. "We have to distinguish between machine learning, where the computer "learns" and 'computerized learning,' where the computer is used as an aid to learning via the running of software that..."

Dan broke in. "And how is machine learning connected to data mining? It sounds pretty ambiguous to someone not familiar with it."

"That's an important point, Dan. We can denote two parallel areas of machine learning: data mining and pattern recognition. Many of the tools and algorithms developed for machine learning are shared in both fields."

"So, what is the ultimate goal of machine learning? What is it supposed to do?" Evyatar interjected.

"The main goal of machine learning is computer processing of real-world data to solve a specific problem. It's used when it is not possible to write a computer program for the problem. The goal of the learning can be modeling, predicting, or discovering facts about the real world. Speech recognition systems can also use machine learning to learn from the syllable patterns that produced them."

"...And with the use of deepfake technology," Gideon also decided to intervene. Correct me if I'm wrong..."

"You're not wrong. You correctly touched on a critical point, Gideon," replied Eric, "And we have already seen the combination of the issues that Noam supports with machine learning."

"And what about data mining?" said Evyatar, "How does it fit in? Can you explain that?"

"Data mining is running an algorithm to uncover information contained in existing databases. It's a process designed to explore and quickly analyze a massive amount of information by automated means," said Eric.

"We could stay here for hours benefitting from Eric's knowledge," Dan concluded, "but we'll have time for completing his review at the team's general meeting. I am sure this will be a key step in understanding the technological threats and this issue of Russian aid to Iran."

Chapter 21

TEHRAN

General Kashani and Dr. Madani were called to the Iranian president's office for an urgent discussion at which the situation of the country's economy was revealed to be close to bankruptcy. There is no certainty, the president's economic advisers argued, that the sanctions will be lifted. Even if they are renewed with the participation of the United States, it is not clear what the effects of the agreement between the six powers and Iran will be.

"The supreme leader is deeply concerned about the worsening economic situation," the president said to them, "he has demanded to know what we can do about it. This ongoing problem, unfortunately, has recently become even more serious. The leader is going to call a multi-participant meeting and discussion, in order to arrive at a course of action that would alleviate the situation as soon as possible."

"Why don't we seek aid from the Russians and their hackers?" said Madani, "I got the impression from our meetings in Moscow that they would be happy to handle the Americans...and no holds barred."

"You mean the cyber operation on the banks in the United States?" asked the president. "It is an idea I heard about from the commander of the Revolutionary Guard. Can it be carried out?"

"We, in the Quds Force, can offer better solutions than the ones the Revolutionary Guard proposes," protested General Kashani. "Doctor Madani and his scientific team have the ability to think creatively..."

"What exactly do you have in mind? It must be an outstanding proposal in order to be presented to the leader at the meeting. Tell us what you have in mind, Dr. Madani? insisted the president.

"Our scientists are capable of activating a series of commands to transfer huge sums from numerous banks in the United States and into our hands. And this perhaps can also be done with banks of other countries in the West," replied Madani, "In addition, we have gained some knowledge about blockchain technology; the use of Bitcoin to transfer funds almost without limits or restrictions and without exposing the source of the actions."

"I suggest we leave it to Dr. Madani and his people. They have experience in these new technologies," Kashani intervened, "I hope you understand, Honorable President, and have no doubt that we know well the technologies which could resolve our national economic distress."

"Your approach makes sense. I will ask you to present the idea of how to obtain the funds to the supreme leader, Dr. Madani." concluded the president.

***

Kashani and Madani left the meeting with the president in good spirits. However, they knew the real challenge would be to gain the supreme leader's support at the upcoming meeting. Kashani stressed that the leader needed to be absolutely convinced that their plan was superior to any which the Revolutionary Guard would propose.

"We have an advantage over the Revolutionary Guard," said Madani. "Our relationship with Putin and the top echelon of the Russian government. They will help us to a certain extent with technological support above and beyond what we have received in the past few years from North Korea."

***

The supreme leader opened the meeting:

"Our beloved republic is in a financial crisis. Much of our economy has been severely affected by the latest sanctions imposed on us by Trump." All those attending listened intently to his words. "The sanctions are hurting us badly," the leader continued in a louder voice than usual, "and there is growing fear of a rebellion by the middle-class. Fortunately, they have not yet taken to the streets. I have asked you, therefore, as the leaders of our republic, to come together and find ways of obtaining the necessary funds to extricate us from this trouble."

"We have considered several options that can deal with our financial distress," Madani began with confidence as the leader nodded his head and encouraged him to be the one to continue the discussion. "Our scientists at the Quds Force have several possible strategies that can funnel significant sums from a large number of banks in the United States. In addition, our economists have studied blockchain technology and the use of Bitcoin to transfer large sums of money without exposing the fact that we are doing this..."

The commander of the Revolutionary Guard quickly broke in: "We have not heard, Honorable Leader, of using Bitcoin as a decentralized currency with the capacity to save us," he grumbled, "Our economists point to it as only theoretical at this time. Why are Dr. Madani's young sages so confident about such an impulsive and outlandish operation that has yet to be tested?" asked the commander, without wiping the sneer off his face.

"If I may," General Kashani addressed the supreme leader, "I would like to highlight our excellent relations with Russia. No one doubts the cyber capabilities and talent of the Russian hackers. When looking at the knowhow of using decentralized currencies, Russia leads in the field. It is important also to point out Dr. Madani obtained the Russians' consent to maintain our ties with North Korea both by virtue of their status among the cyber powers and their proven nuclear capability. I am sure, Your Honor, that Madani and his young researchers, with Russian and North Korean support will be able to resolve our economic crisis."

After several more minutes of heated discussion, the supreme leader called for silence and declared: "I accept the recommendations of Dr. Madani and the Quds Force." This was his conclusion despite all the objections of the commander of the Revolutionary Guard.

"Our relationship with Russia is precious and essential." The leader turned to General Kashani and Dr. Madani. "I fully expect that you will know how to protect and preserve it and thus enable us to receive the full support that Russia can provide." The supreme leader ended the meeting.

Chapter 22

TEHRAN AND PYONGYANG

General Kashani was agitated and wanted Madani to tell him about the preparations for the financial cyber operation the supreme leader had approved. It would be the most important mission the Quds Force had ever undertaken to plan and also carry out.

"What is happening? We promised the leader to prepare everything for the plan as soon as possible!" Kashani exclaimed even before Madani had a chance to sit down. "The future of the Quds Force depends a great deal on the success of completing this operation quickly, on schedule. I again do not need to remind you that the Revolutionary Guard are waiting for us to make the slightest error in the plan or a delay in carrying out the mission. That is what we promised the leader. Don't the Russians understand the urgency and our need for their assistance? And what about North Korea? You yourself said that Russia would not object to continuing our technological collaboration with them."

"Yes, commander. The Russians are aware of the pressure we are under and the urgency to complete the planning. Regarding North Korea, I wanted to update you. They have requested our help in uranium enrichment technology."

"Did they contact you? When? What do they want?"

"They had repeated malfunctions in the operation of their centrifuges, similar to the problems we had when the Stuxnet computer worm paralyzed our facilities in Natanz. I thought I would go to Pyongyang and take with me our nuclear scientist colleague from Pakistan, Dr. Abdul Qadir Khan. If you approve, this would be an opportunity to consult with General Lee about the technological aspects of our cyber-attack on the US banks."

"I see. All right, Madani, I will approve that you can, with an aide or two, go meet with the North Koreans on the condition that it does not take more than a day or two."

***

Madani and the Pakistani doctor's first day of the visit dealt with malfunctions in the centrifuge arrays for uranium enrichment. During the tests, Dr. Al-Qadir Khan discovered a familiar computer virus. It was removed by General Lee himself, to the delight of the scientists in North Korea.

"Well, Madani my friend," General Lee Hong-Jik began as they sat in his office for a private meeting Madani had requested. "Thank you for the successful handling of our centrifuge malfunction. Abdul Qadir Khan is an impressive professional. It is no wonder he receives so much support from the president of Pakistan."

"Yes, General Lee, I learned from you that the key to success is in choosing the right people to work with. What we saw in the handling of the malfunction at the centrifuge plant proves it."

The one-on-one meeting yielded surprising and positive results. Madani shared with General Lee, with full frankness, the supreme leader's instructions to finally carry out the revenge on the United States for Soleimani's murder. Now, Madani added, we must also avenge the painful assassination of the nuclear scientist. The Mossad and the CIA are responsible for these crimes and they must be avenged. The general listened to Madani's review, who literally begged for advice and support for an operation the Americans 'couldn't possible conceive of' and a punishment for Israel for the murder of Iran's nuclear scientists and the repeated attacks on Iran's nuclear facilities.

"Perhaps you should pattern your plan by what the British company 'Cambridge Analytica' did to enable Russia to change American positions to help elect Donald Trump as president of the United States?"

General Lee noted that with the use of technology that 'Cambridge Analytica' developed, it is not possible to link with Facebook after it became an open platform and not a closed social network.

"On our last visit to Russia, we heard about the activity on social networks, but they did not go into detail. On the other hand, we learned ways of obtaining financing to ease our economic crisis, which has been aggravated by the sanctions initiated by the United States. They affected not only us in Iran but also Russia, following its involvement in Ukraine. The European Union also joined in the sanctions. However, the Russians gave us information about new tools to extricate ourselves from the economic pressures."

"What exactly? What were the Russians talking about? Can you elaborate?" asked the general.

"Yes, they gave us authorization to talk to you about the economic issues and the ways to deal with them. According to the Russians, Artificial Intelligence and cyber operations allow them to penetrate banks in the United States and the West in general. With deepfake, we have a tool that gives us options for withdrawing funds. For example, you click on a news clip and see the president of the United States at a press conference with a foreign leader. The dialogue seems real, the press conference also looks real and everyone sees it. Only later do you learn that the president's head was transposed on someone else's body and none of what was shown ever actually happened."

"Interesting, Madani. You should know that we have also done a great deal of research with regards to obtaining funding in original ways, including using deepfake..."

"Ah, General Lee, my friend, you are in a very suitable position for our needs in dealing with the Great Satan, the United States, and the Little Satan, the Zionist entity. You would agree, I believe that we are a triumvirate: North Korea, Russia, and Iran – all with identical goals and new technological tools."

"I want to mention again the issue of changing public attitude with the aid of manipulating social networks in the United States," replied General Lee. "This is of great importance in the research efforts of our Cyber University, where our best hackers are deployed. The researchers there are preparing to 'bring the United States to its knees.' You are welcome to visit the university again with your people and learn about the potential for carrying out combined operations."

"Thank you, general, my friend," replied Madani expressing his gratitude at the general's words. "I would be most happy to visit your hacker university again. As we have in the past, I am sure we will learn important things there that we did not know before."

***

On the return flight from Beijing to Tehran, Madani and his young assistants continued analyzing the information they'd garnered in the meetings with the North Koreans. Madani enjoyed the assistants' enthusiasm and curiosity, which would be needed for the final formulation of plans to deal with the economic problem. At the same time, Madani knew they must have a superior plan, better than anything the Revolutionary Guard could present. Overall, he was glad to point out that North Korea remained a loyal and great friend; while Russia also continued its significant support to help cope with Iran's economic sanctions problems, and at the same time, also help in the planning of painful revenge against the American and Israeli enemies.

Chapter 23

TEL AVIV

Gideon and Nimer responded quickly to Evyatar's summoning them. "We are on top of internal communications of Iran's top brass. There appears to be an unusual struggle between the Revolutionary Guard leadership and the Quds Force. Both organizations want to be in charge of the solution to the hardships incurred by the economic sanctions which the United States recently imposed on Iran."

"This isn't the first time that these two groups are fighting for leadership and prestige; and to have control of financial resources," commented Nimer. "The balance of power changed after General Soleimani was eliminated. Kashani, the new commander of the Quds Force, has not yet proven that he can step into his shoes. Normally, even when Soleimani was alive, the Revolutionary Guard controlled the entirety of Iran's budget and actually dictated policies to the supreme leader and the President of the Republic."

"Can we hear more details on what is particularly troubling to the Iranians about the sanctions?" Noam interjected, "Ah, here is Doctor Deutsch. Welcome," she exclaimed. "We should get into the heart of the financial problems you spoke of immediately after breaking into Iranian communications. We also were active outside of Iran, especially regarding Russia's strategies."

"Right as usual, Noam," interjected Evyatar, "I'm going to ask Eric, who has already filled us in on a significant part of his analysis, to describe what the Iranians actually intend to do."

"There is no doubt the issue is top priority in Iran since the supreme leader is involved and pushing for moves to solve the economic crisis. In the struggle at the top of the administration, it appears that the Quds Force has taken the lead. Dr. Madani is responsible for initiating the plan he presented to the president and the supreme leader."

"What do we currently know about Madani's plan?" asked Dieter who was proud of his son's place of honor in Evyatar's surveillance team. "And what will be required to thwart the success of the program?"

"Already at an early stage of the program, we spotted bank orders that we are certain were clearly fake. They were probably testing their ability to withdraw much larger amounts in the future..."

"How did Iran gain that capacity? They haven't had it until now." Nimer continued, "Iran did not have such advanced cyber tools previously. Is it due to North Korea, which has in the past passed on advanced technological knowledge to Iran?"

"The significant player is Russia, which has been helping Iran in all economic cyber issues. The quarrels at the top revealed interesting and crucial details in the plan put forth by the Quds Force headed by Madani. We have seen intentions of using deepfake technology and also an alarming dialogue between the Quds Force and Russian scientists to use blockchain and bitcoin to acquire funds without anyone being able to identify their source and for whom they are intended."

"Don't forget, gentlemen," commented Dan, "North Korea's continuous support for providing Iran with knowledge of AI and cyber technologies. Without their assistance, Iran would not be where it is vis-a-vis the great powers."

"If you will allow me," Deutsch interjected, "I am certain this must also worry the United States. I intend to inform their various agencies of what we have just heard from Eric."

"Right. These are serious threats Eric has pointed out," Gideon asserted, "Even in the few issues presented to us, there are challenges that require a lot of work. I have no doubt that finding an effective countermeasure plan is our most important and pressing challenge. Nimer and I will update Nahari, the head of Mossad, with what we have heard here. Dan, Evyatar, Noam, and Eric must leave and formulate a detailed proposal to thwart the economic plan that is taking shape in Iran."

***

"I would like to draw your attention to new developments in Tehran," Evyatar spoke when all the members of the extended team gathered in the surveillance room. "We have uncovered new developments, thanks to our enhanced monitoring ability. We have access to the communications between Madani and General Kashani and also what they are hearing from the supreme leader.

I found it appropriate to bring up the issue, which appears to be a concrete security threat, at the weekly meeting of the extended team. Eric and I recommend that we assess the degree of risk and determine which action to take. Noam and Dan are already deep into the issues and we should hear from them."

"Evyatar passed on information to Noam and me, which is not entirely clear at this point, about preparations being made by the Quds Force in Iran for a mega-operation that will be aided by innovative communication technology. In our opinion, this is further proof of the success of the algorithm system developed by Cambridge Analytica.

The system, according to findings of the FBI, was operated by the Russians, managed to manipulate millions of Americans into voting for Trump for the presidency. The system relies on algorithms developed by Artificial Intelligence," said Eric.

"I get the impression that Iran's intentions are much more than manipulating social networks with Cambridge Analytica against the United States and Israel," Noam interjected.

"We have heard about Iran's progress, in coordination with Nasrallah and the military arm of Hezbollah, and the Quds Force, along with North Korea. Each of these groups is involved in one way or another in the planning of the major operation that the supreme Iranian leader ordered the Quds Force to carry out. This is in retaliation for the chain of operations, attacks on personnel and facilities in Iran by Israel with the assistance of the United States. We have observed two different types of actions here, one is the use of attack tunnels to take an Israeli soldier captive and even take control of a settlement in the north, while the other action is something more generally Iranian called 'digital warfare.'

"The name requires clarification. What do we know about this digital warfare?" Evyatar posed the question.

"Countries all over the world are, in practice, waging digital warfare, which is actually an attack on attitudes and consciousness. Instead of missiles, bombs, tanks, and planes, these countries, with the help of the digital technology giants, Facebook, Google, Amazon, and Apple, are user-friendly, popular, and optimistic technologies. Their goal is to 'connect you to your friends,' and also 'make the world a better place' with technologies that capture our attention all our waking hours. It seems that it is easier for the giants of digital technology to infiltrate the minds of the general public thanks to the 'positive' types of messages they transmit."

Let me understand," Gideon intervened for the first time, "What do we actually know about this major attack, the one you picked up on recently, the one the supreme leader ordered? What does it have to do with their dealing with the economic crisis? And in addition, we have not heard details about the operation planned as a response to the recent attacks as well as the assassination of Soleimani. It's also not clear," Gideon went on without stopping, "what would be considered by Iran as a fitting punishment for the sabotage at their nuclear facilities? And we need updates regarding the political-military-technological aid Iran intends to receive from Russia and North Korea. Lastly, my young friends, you talked about Hamas tunnels on the border of the Gaza Strip and the ones dug on the northern border. We have not heard specifics, only a general description. Can we have more details? Otherwise, it will be hard to know how to build countermeasures."

There was silence in the surveillance room where the series of questions Gideon raised were reverberating. Dan, Evyatar, Noam, and Eric exchanged glances. Finally, Evyatar spoke up.

"You're correct in pointing out the entire range of targets that Iran has apparently decided to take action against. We do not yet know their priorities and if they can run several of these planned operations at the same time. For now, after overcoming the malfunctions of listening in on their communication networks, we are learning things that will help us get an idea of their priorities. What concerns them the most? The economic situation caused by the sanctions. At the same time, I would not underestimate the importance of the image Iran wants to convey. Their response to our attacks on major figures like Soleimani and the damage inflicted on their nuclear facilities must be at the heart of their 'great' operation...I see that Deutsch wants to say something about the US sanctions."

Evyatar stopped and gave the floor to Deutsch.

"Yes. With your permission, I want to comment on the sanctions, especially those that the US imposed, and when they will be in effect until. It is also important to state some truths regarding Russia's intervention in several areas in our region," continued Deutsch.

"These are important issues," said Gideon, and Dieter nodded in enthusiastic agreement, "and we should hear what Deutsch has to say."

"There is no doubt that the sanctions are effective," continued Deutsch, "and they have already brought Iran unprecedented inflation. We have heard this from the surveillance of Evyatar's team. Russia's interference in US social networks was investigated and found to be related to the relations between Russia and the United States with no connection to Iran. We mention here the Russian involvement in Ukraine and the sanctions that the United States and the European Union countries have imposed on it. But, gentlemen, let's acknowledge Iran's ability to withstand economic pressure, mainly from the Americans. It is beyond what we expected."

"There is a difference between what the leadership in Iran broadcasts and the dire plight they are actually in; and that demands they desperately search for solutions to the economic situation to close this gap," Dieter intervened in the discussion. "I can make out the Revolutionary Guard's concern about the unrest of the middle class which has so far avoided putting up real opposition to the rule of the Ayatollahs. It is clear that this major operation they are talking about will include something to either negate or at least reduce the effect of the sanctions."

"If the economic distress comes to be seen as an existential threat to Iran," Dan joined the discussion, "we should focus on planning actions that will prevent Iran from trying anything to reduce the economic pressure on them. Revenge for the assassination of key Iranian figures would not be what they would consider as existential threats. It is precisely the reduction of aid to the Syrian regime and the restraint of attacks against American forces stationed in Iraq, in my opinion, that can tempt Iran. I will add, following on from Deutsch's words, that we must not forget Russia's part in this; its assistance to Iran at this stage of formulating their responses."

"If we are already mentioning the Gaza Strip border and the northern border with Hezbollah," insisted Noam, "we saw what happened after the kidnapping of one soldier, Gilad Shalit, and the hundreds of terrorists we had to release. Not to mention, if God forbid, they manage to take over an entire settlement."

"Noam is right," Gideon began summing up the meeting, "and it is also important to deal with the attack tunnels Iran will try to use, as part of thwarting their 'great' operation that we still don't know enough about. Thanks to Gideon, Noam, Eric, and especially Evyatar for the important information. We will update Nahari and complete the preparations to counter the major operation being prepared by Iran, assisted by Russia and North Korea."

***

Nahari rose to greet Gideon and Dieter, smiling and shaking their hands. They both appreciated the trust which the head of the Mossad had in his senior advisors.

"Evyatar, Dan, Noam, and the other young people in the extended team have been able to listen in on a great number of conversations and consultations, mainly between the Iranians, but also to information transmitted by Hezbollah and the Syrians..."

"To what extent?" Nahari exclaimed in the reactive style that Gideon and Dieter had learned to expect, "Any new things you didn't know?"

"We knew about some of it and some of it was new to us, but it is important to emphasize the large number of topics and the connection between them," explained Gideon.

"I am happy to point out Dieter's role in interpreting the various dialogues between the Iranian leaders and Hezbollah. Thanks to him, we were able to better assess their priorities in formulating their next moves. We learned not only about their way of dealing with the sanctions and the difficult economic situation they've caused, but also about their intention to carry out a mega-operation led by the Quds Force. One of the new issues is the development of a supersonic cruise missile that the Russians are supplying the technological basis for. It's a missile similar to the Kh-47M2 Kinzhal missile which Russia has recently perfected..."

"That is really new for me," said Nahari, "Why did

the Russians deviate from their policy of not providing, even to friendly countries, advanced technological systems so soon?"

"Good question, Nahari, it is indeed unusual," Dieter confirmed, "Gideon and I received information about a special project and we intend to find out where it's heading. But besides what Gideon has described so far," Dieter continued, "there is a wide range of issues, which we have already uncovered, of the possibilities of using attack tunnels both on the border of the Gaza Strip with Hamas, and on the northern border with Hezbollah."

"That is fact," confirmed Gideon, "and we know that Dieter is the most knowledgeable of all of us on the issue of the tunnels."

Nahari continued to press his two senior advisors with questions for several minutes and concluded by giving them the green light to continue preparations to thwart Iranian activity in all the fields presented.

Chapter 24

MOSCOW

President Putin and the Russian elite were called to the operations room in the Politburo where extensive activity by the Israeli Air Force was being watched on the monitors.

Foreign Minister Sergey Lavrov addressed Putin.

"Sir, recently we were informed that Israel had agreed to curtail bombing strategic targets in Syria and the Iranian forces there, which are assisting the Syrian regime. There were negotiations to that effect between the Russian and Israeli Air Force commanders. However, Honorable President, The Israeli Air Force is continually attacking our convoys that are transporting anti-tank weapon systems and precision missiles to the Syrians and to Hezbollah. These are unprecedented attacks," the minister ardently exclaimed.

"What kind of arrangement was made between the air forces?" asked Putin.

"We agreed with the Israeli Air Force that they would notify us in advance of all their activity in Syrian and Lebanese airspace" the Russian Air Force commander spoke up. "In this case, the Israelis announced the attack only a few minutes before it began."

"With your permission, Mr. President," interjected the Russian defense minister. "What we have here significantly exceeds the scope of such an agreement the commander speaks of. This is not tactical, but strategic and political in character. It is fitting, Honorable President, to protest this violation in the harshest terms to Israel, but more than that," the defense minister continued, "the United States, which supports Israel's activities, needs also to be restrained."

"I concur with the defense minister," said Lavrov. "And I would like to stress that the Americans are backing the Israeli moves and we ought to let them know that they have gone too far. Perhaps we should support Donald Trump once again for a second term as president."

"I would like to hear from the director of the Federal Security Bureau, General Banikov," Putin cut in, "what can you add to this, Viktor?"

"Honorable President, we are constantly tracking developments vis-à-vis the United States," replied the head of the FSB. Our involvement in the presidential election in the United States exposed our propaganda mechanism, which soon came to be called 'fake news.' Ahead of the new elections, the director of the NSA warned of our deliberate and aggressive campaign that you yourself led, Mr. President. US intelligence, they say, has spotted thousands of our automated systems, robots as well as human teams, a network of websites, and fake profiles that streamed heavily slanted messages and helped get Trump elected. Russia, US intelligence officials have stated, has succeeded in using Facebook and Google to undermine the trust of the American public in a seemingly 'democratic' process."

"Interesting, Viktor, and alarming," commended Putin, "Why have we been so exposed? What will we do without the intelligence-gathering infrastructure we have built up with great effort over the past years? How do we proceed in our struggle for control over what happens in the United States? Who has ideas of what we need to do now?

How do we respond to Israel's current activity that goes beyond anything we have known to date? Comrade Foreign Minister, maybe you can tell us?!" roared Putin.

"The answer lies with Iran, Your Honor, and its drive to increase the presence of its forces in Syria. This was the initiative of General Soleimani, the former commander of the Quds Force who was killed by an American attack drone. It was part of a comprehensive plan by the general to achieve Shiite supremacy in the Middle East and the entire world..."

"What has that to do with what I want to know?" Putin continued to pressure him. "Only we can convince Iran not to increase the size of its forces in Syria. I would rather reduce them and let Israel see that we can influence matters in their favor."

"Your Honor," the defense minister ventured, "I don't think we can rely on negotiations. The Israelis only understand power and that's how we must deal with them. It would be wrong to pressure Iran to reduce its forces in Syria. They represent an important part of our policy in the region. Without support for Assad's regime, we will lose the only port we have in the Mediterranean..."

"You still have not clarified, Comrade Minister of Defense, what the appropriate response is to the activities of the Israeli Air Force. How do you strengthen the defense of both Iran and Syria – and of course Hezbollah – against the threats from Israel and the United States? My decision is to continue to take action on all fronts: against the threats of the Israeli attacks in Syria and Lebanon, upgrading the supersonic missiles on the Iranian front, and continuing to refine technology," concluded Putin, thus ending the discussion.

Chapter 25

WASHINGTON

Deutsch was once again called to Washington for consultations. In a short phone conversation with his friend the deputy director of the CIA before he left for Washington, he learned about the unease over recent information the FBI had received concerning Russian voter manipulation on American social network platforms. All the intelligence agencies, the deputy director said, were deeply bothered by Russia's interference in public opinion in the United States and its influence on results of the congressional and presidential elections. There were other issues on the agenda, said the deputy, but it would be inappropriate to list them even by properly encrypted means...and he ended the call.

***

When Deutsch arrived at the meeting in Washington, he discovered that the first two hours would be devoted to a comprehensive review by CIA personnel, during which they shared their apprehension regarding the

Russia-Iran-North Korea triumvirate. Deutsch listened to details of the technological advances that put North Korea's hacking capabilities at the disposal of all three of the nations that threaten the United States and Israel.

"As you have heard, Dr. Deutsch, North Korea continues to be a cyber-power both for defensive and offensive purposes," the deputy noted. "It was already a strategic threat," he warned, "but the sanctions we imposed on it for refusing to stop their continuing development of nuclear weapons, forces them to sell their technology to the highest bidder..."

"Yes," agreed Deutsch, "We know about the massive marketing operation of their long-range missile technology, cyber capabilities, and even their expertise in the construction of tunnels. Iran, Saudi Arabia, and Libya are among the beneficiaries of these North Korean developments."

"At least we haven't seen them sharing nuclear weapons secrets with other countries, Deutsch, but maybe Israel has other information?"

"No, my friend, I know that not even Israel knows of any intention by North Korea to transfer nuclear technology to Iran despite its attempts to obtain it. According to Israeli intelligence, China, Russia, and even India and Pakistan are also refusing transfer of these technologies to any other country. But you hinted at a Russian threat in our phone conversation. Did you mean to tell me about it face to face?"

"Absolutely, Deutsch. It's important to note that this is related both to the uses of advanced AI technology and the presidential elections in the United States. You will hear later in your meetings at NSA and at the Pentagon about the disturbing cooperation between the Russia-North Korea-Iran axis on the subject of aid to Iran. The aid also deals with uranium enrichment for their nuclear facilities, and especially protecting them from cyber-attacks that have been directed against them. We have to keep in mind Israel's concerns about Russia's military and political aid to Syria and the presence of Iranian forces there."

"It seems to me that there are many issues on the burner about aid to Iran and there are those who are stirring the pot, such as Russian intrusion on social media and in our elections. I wonder what kind of stew will come out of all of this." Deutsch pondered aloud.

"Good point, my friend. Let's meet again after your other meetings – better just the two of us – and we'll get a clearer picture of where we're headed."

***

Deutsch had subsequent talks with senior NSA officials regarding Russian interference in the US presidential elections. He witnessed surprising close collaboration between the NSA and the FBI that led to the exposure of Russian agents who had been dormant until recently. These people were called into action, FBI officials claimed, on direct orders from Putin. They were trained for aggressive covert action on social media networks in the US, urging Americans to distrust their federal government.

"It's good to be here with you. I feel comfortable and welcome," said Deutsch, "You always have something new for us and it's important to discuss these burning issues with you. But first I want to call your attention to the impressive achievements of Dan Avni's 'New Future' enterprise. The company operates in Silicon Valley and has a successful ongoing relationship with the SRI Institute that I manage, and that of course, adds to their ability to perform important research for you."

"I am up to date on that, my friend. I know there has already been an appeal from the head of the CIA to his counterpart in Israel, Nahari, the head of the Mossad. There is an agreement in principle, which is also accepted by the Ministry of Defense, to act jointly to thwart the interventions of the unholy 'threesome.' They are set to defend against Russian interference, particularly in our elections, and in the long term, but no less to defend against the threatening issue of Russian aid in the development of advanced AI technology in Iran."

"The Israelis are closely following what's happening in Iran and Syria as well as Russian and Ukrainian activity," affirmed Deutsch, "It is interesting to see that both Russia and Iran are subject to economic sanctions spearheaded by the United States. Iran is under greater pressure after President Trump withdrew from the nuclear deal on Iran with the six powers. And the United States and the European Union, as we know, are punishing Russia for its aggression in Ukraine."

"A good point," commented the deputy, "So there is a common denominator here on the damaging effect of the economic sanctions?

"Exactly," confirmed Deutsch, "and this connects to the other issues, such as aid to Syria and allowing Iran to introduce military forces into the conflict, all of which encourages Russia to act, although not openly, against America and Israel."

"We are at the crossroads of important decisions, and our cooperation with Israel is essential," the deputy continued, "We are mainly concerned with Russia's attempt to sway public opinion and influence our democratic system abusing social networks as we saw in our election. But I know you have meetings scheduled with the FBI and you will hear details from them about their analysis of the findings on the extensive operations of the Russians here in our backyard."

For a long while, Deutsch listened to the deputy's comprehensive overview of the agency's efforts to use the human factor as sources of information, something that had been somewhat neglected in recent years. The activity of terrorist organizations in the Middle East, noted the deputy, is not fully clear to the intelligence organizations in the US. Deutsch's involvement in the war on terror in the Middle East and Iran made him an important intelligence source.

"We greatly appreciate the contribution of the SRI Institute and also the welcome activity of Dan Avni's 'New Future' company in Silicon Valley. This will definitely help in facing the challenges that Moscow presents."

"Thank you, my friend," said Deutsch, "for an instructive lesson. You've helped me a lot and I'm better prepared for my meeting with the FBI. I am maintaining my good relationship with the Mossad and of course I will make certain that you and the NSA both keep a good, open relationship with the Mossad. Cooperation in the war against the common enemy coupled with mutual respect will, in my opinion, guide all of us."

***

A security escort vehicle was waiting for Deutsch in front of the entrance of the main CIA building at Langley. The CIA deputy went out of his way to accompany Deutsch to the car. In addition to the driver, Deutsch noticed two security guards in the vehicle and was surprised at the level of security the FBI had ordered for his visit. The agency's headquarters were in Washington, in the J. Edgar Hoover building, named in honor of the organization's revered but controversial first director.

***

"Doctor Deutsch, we have a hint of some activity of an Israeli spy cell and we are not sure if it is an actual threat. It appears to have a broad digital signature and we are still not clear if this is an Iranian duplicitous initiative and what Russia has to do with all of it. At this point we thought to inform only you and through you only Mr. Nahari, of the Mossad. Now let's get to the heart of the Russian problem as we see it. Russia's connection to Iran and Syria is not to be minimized. As you will hear, the Federal Bureau of Investigation views

Russian activity with great concern; it affects the very core of our society..."

"Indeed, sir, I have heard about this only in general terms in the conversation I had with the CIA yesterday about Putin's moves. It is clear that maintaining the security of your democracy is absolutely essential. This issue also concerns Israel, which is extremely troubled by the combination of predatory Russian policy and its cooperation with Israel's enemies in the Middle East. But don't let me stop you, please continue."

"Right. We know from our surveillance that Russian agents intruded on social networks. Facebook, Twitter, and Google are all infected with data and videos that went viral and their source leads back to Moscow at the highest level. Our intelligence community concluded that the Russian government definitely interfered in the recent US election. We determined that Russian President Vladimir Putin himself ordered an 'influence' campaign targeting the results of the election. The goals were to undermine public confidence in the democratic processes in the States, to defame former Secretary of State and Democratic presidential candidate, Hillary Clinton, and impair her chances. Beyond computer hacking and cyberattacks, the campaign included spreading fake news that was often disseminated through the social networks," concluded the head of the investigative agency.

"But Trump won the election and it's already behind us. What is there left to do now?" asked Deutsch.

"True, the election results are behind us, but Putin was so impressed by the success of the manipulation that we don't think that's the end of the story. The strategy of using social networks, cyber-attacks and advanced AI may also be going on in the Middle East. More important still, is that the NSA head and FBI top brass jointly stated in Washington that Russia had hacked the computers at the Democratic National Committee headquarters, as well as the email account of Hillary Clinton's campaign chairman, and fed all the data to WikiLeaks. By all accounts, this is a serious blow to the democratic process that must be added to our agenda."

As the conversation with the head of the Bureau continued, Deutsch found the man open to hearing Deutsch's assessments of the situation in the Middle East. Russia's support for the Alawite regime of Bashir Assad together with its turning of a blind eye to the Iranian incursion into Syria, was emphasized by Deutsch as a grave danger to the State of Israel.

***

On Deutsch's return from Washington he immediately asked for a meeting with Nahari.

"I have heard already from my friends in Washington that your visit was a success and that you represented our perspective very well there," Nahari complimented him. "I've asked Gideon and Dieter to join us."

Deutsch immediately described to them all his meetings with the head of the FBI in Washington on the suspicions, which were not yet substantiated, of a spy cell that supposedly began working for Israel. He also described the Americans' desire for concrete assistance, not just intelligence, from Israel. Gideon and Dieter pointed to another fact, which they believed should be kept in mind: Russia's commitment to bolster the Assad regime in Syria with the help of the Iranian Quds Force.

Dieter further stated that Hezbollah was providing critically important military support to the Syrian president and his regime by sending Hezbollah fighters into the civil war in Syria. Gideon emphasized the importance of Hezbollah's participation in the fighting, pointing out that they had become a real army and not 'just' a terrorist organization whose main activity is attacks on Israel. Dieter added his evaluation of the training that the Revolutionary Guard and the Quds Force provide to Hezbollah's military arm. He explained that it is highly advantageous for Iran to have a trained military body that assumes responsibility, even a strategic one, in the Middle East region.

Deutsch, true to his promise in the meeting with the heads of the US intelligence organizations, had prepared a comprehensive review for Nahari and the staff of the Mossad about the findings on Russia's activities. The important part of the review was the American assessment of Israel's ability to understand the Russians' way of thinking.

He recommended the integration of the research team of wiretapping and cyber assaults that Evyatar lead, to work in conjunction with the Americans. His opinion was that the cooperation of Mossad and the intelligence division of the IDF, with the intelligence organizations of the United States against the Russians was not only possible, but highly desirable.

***

Deutsch joined the weekly update in Nahari's office with the two NSA personnel stationed at the American Embassy in Israel. A piece of information had just reached Nahari from listening in on Iran's networks. They were planning to use newly developed technologies against Israel.

"I understand, Deutsch that these are global issues and are not just about Russian support for Syria and its assistance to Iran in deploying Iranian fighters there."

"That is absolutely correct, Nahari. The Russians are staging a worldwide strategic operation. There is the interference on social networks in the United States and an attempt to undermine democracy there, and Russia's turbulent relationship with Ukraine after the annexation of the Crimean peninsula and the city of Sevastopol on the Black Sea coast, the largest and most important city on the entire Crimean peninsula..."

"But let's not forget Russia's categorical failure in Afghanistan. It retreated with its tail between its legs, and also in the conflict that is still ongoing against Chechen terrorism," commented Gideon, "and the annexation of the Crimean Peninsula and the support for citizens of Russian origin in Ukraine brought economic sanctions down on them by the US and countries of the European Union." said Gideon.

"Gideon is right," confirmed Nahari, "and there is

of course, Russia's substantial aid to the Syrian regime and Assad, and the defense with the missile batteries aimed at the Israeli Air Force sorties…"

"If I may interject," broke in Dieter, "we need to also take into account Russian technological capabilities with attack drones, the missiles that are being transported to Hezbollah in Lebanon, and the Russians' capabilities in Artificial Intelligence and cyber-attack. But there is a new wild card in the Russians' deck. The supersonic cruise missiles that we heard about only recently from Putin himself. This is a weapons capability we haven't seen until now."

"Deutsch, what do the intelligence organizations expect from us?" asked Nahari. "What can little Israel do in trying to stop the Russians from becoming a global power once again, something they have been striving to do for some time. How widespread and dangerous a threat is all of this?"

"I am just getting to that, Nahari, which is the icing on the cake from my meetings with our intelligence organizations. We're talking about the human factor in Israel, the large community of more than a million Russians who immigrated to Israel in the last several decades. The Americans claim that even with all their information gathering ability, with all their top level technology, only the Israelis with Russian origins can grasp the Russian psyche and be of real benefit to them. I promised them to bring this up with you, Nahari, and I strongly recommend our helping them."

The meeting lasted for over an hour, with Nahari managing to navigate and reach an understanding and agreement on every issue. He asked Deutsch to let the American intelligence organizations know that Israel was willing to continue further strengthening its strategic cooperation with the US.

Chapter 26

TEL AVIV

"Good morning, Evyatar. What have you found out?" Nahari turned to Evyatar at a meeting with Nahari, along with Gideon and Dieter the senior advisors.

"We were able to intercept exchanges between the Quds Force and the Revolutionary Guard in their discussions with the supreme leader. It's now clear that Iran is set on a revenge operation, especially after Hezbollah's failure in the attack on Ya'ara near the northern border."

"And what is your takeaway from all of this? Where does it lead us?" Nahari pressed Evyatar.

"I would work on that conflict between the Revolutionary Guard and the Quds Force." Dieter added, "The rift between those two dangerous organizations could give us an advantage in our countermeasure operations."

"Yes." Evyatar began, "From what we have gathered from the gist of the issues the Iranians are discussing, it's our impression that so far, the Quds Force has the edge. From the perspective of the advancement of technology, we see a greatly increased use of drones, both the small ones like our 'wasps' and the larger attack drones, which are armed with missiles. But the really dangerous threat is the new supersonic cruise missile Iran is developing, with significant technological support from Russia. They are working on their own version of the high-speed missiles that are immune to interception by existing means of detection."

"And what do we know about the use of Artificial Intelligence and its derivatives in conjunction with this big operation they're planning?" Gideon joined in, "We've seen Iran using cyber-attacks for some time now, and they are no doubt continuing with that.

"We also know for certain that this time around they'll have missiles that are ten times faster than the speed of sound. These Russian cruise missiles are launched from MiG-31 or Sukhoi 57 aircraft. It appears that communication with the missile, including transmitting the precise location of the target is made before the missile separates from the plane and is launched."

"We need to address an important question before you continue with more about the great 'Revenge' operation," Nahari insisted, "Have you any idea of Iran's planned target? Do you have more than just a general reference to a revenge attack on the United States and Israel?"

"No, Nahari, only the intent to hit at important figures such as what happened with Iran and the assassination of Soleimani and the senior nuclear scientist. We'll update you on any additional details we may uncover," promised Evyatar.

"If we go back to the operation Iran is planning," Gideon interjected, "We can assume they will combine AI and cyber-attacks along with the conventional use of drones and cruise missiles. To be clear, we should focus on the deepfake technology Iran has at their disposal."

"Yes, Gideon, but let's remember that these are still just generalities and we will need to do a lot of intelligence gathering and analysis of the findings in order to build a defense against their big operation."

"From everything that has been said here by Evyatar and his team," Nahari concluded, "we have to clearly define areas of work. Regarding the integration of the drones and especially the new cruise missiles, I ask you, Gideon and Dieter, to take this in hand. The issues of cyber and the use of Artificial Intelligence, including deepfake technology, I want Noam and Eric to handle. All the activity will be led by Dan, who will deal with the analysis of the threats and the determination of countermeasures. And you, Evyatar, and your young people," Nahari turned to them, "will continue collecting data to help deal with both the conventional components of the threats and the AI technology. Thank you all. Noam, Dan, and gentlemen, and all of you from Evyatar's team," concluded Nahari, dismissing all the others except for Gideon and Dieter, whom he asked to remain.

"I wanted the three of us to discuss something new that came from the head of the CIA. He said the FBI had talked about a suspected Israeli spy cell in the United States. I didn't believe it was anything serious and I hoped that the FBI would find it was a false alarm after a thorough investigation." Nahari paused and waited for Gideon and Dieter to recall the details of the case that had been brushed aside since they heard about it from Deutsch almost as a side issue. The two advisors looked first at each other and then at Nahari, without a word.

"The head of the CIA was sorry that the FBI could not rule out the possibility of the existence of the cell. We both agreed that we had to deal with the issue. It could seriously damage the fabric of our relationship. I assured him that the Mossad had no knowledge of a spy cell and there was no intention to initiate such an unsuitable thing. We had enough of that with Jonathan Pollard."

"This sounds delusional. It's ridiculous, and it's interesting that the FBI has no concrete evidence of such a spy organization." Gideon argued. "What should we do? I understand that you think that not only Washington, but also Israel needs to find the source of the FBI's contention..."

"If they couldn't uncover if such an organization exists," Dieter added, "we have to assume that there is a sophisticated plot here to 'support' Israel, but to conceal the identity of the supporters. We need to use our best experts in Artificial Intelligence and the entire cyber field, and perhaps also in deepfake and the facial recognition software that Noam developed."

"In my opinion, the ball is more in our court than in the FBI's," said Gideon, "we have an excellent and experienced team, and of course, we can also count on the capabilities of the American intelligence organizations.

And yet, Nahari, I would be careful not to spread this spy cell story to too many others."

"I go along with that," Nahari confirmed with a sigh, "Let's bring this affair to the attention of our teams. We need to unravel this spy cell case quickly."

"Consider it done, Nahari," Gideon and Dieter spoke in unison. "I have complete faith in you," Nahari acknowledged, "and keep on top of Iran's preparations for their 'Great Revenge.' Make sure we don't miss out on a single detail concerning the threat."

Chapter 27

TEHRAN

"I am uneasy about the preparations for the 'Great Revenge' operation we've committed to carry out for the supreme leader," exclaimed General Kashani, waving a sheet of paper with the Revolutionary Guard logo as Doctor Madani entered the room.

"We just received this from the supreme leader's office. The Revolutionary Guard is slandering us with what they call 'repeated failures' that we are keeping from the leader. See what they wrote and tell me what you think our reply should be to the leader about these accusations," Kashani requested, handing Madani the sheet of paper. He scanned it carefully.

"These are lies, as any sane person can see, Commander. There is no problem in composing a suitable answer for the leader," Madani quickly reassured him, pointing to the Revolutionary Guard's sheet. "The design of our version of the Russian Kinzhal supersonic cruise missile is progressing well. It is ahead of the schedule we set with the team of Russian engineers who are supervising our people. Remember, Commander, our Air Force has the MiG 31s that we received from Russia with all the electronic infrastructure necessary for the missiles. This eliminates the need for us to develop a link between the aircraft and the two cruise missiles that the MiG 31 will be equipped with. Blessed be President Putin who approved the transfer of this great technology. It puts us in a central position among the advanced countries in the world," proclaimed Madani.

"The Revolutionary Guard claims that the entire system for the operation we are presenting is not protected and can easily be hacked," said General Kashani, who was still apprehensive.

"This is actually decisive proof of success, Commander, of the security we developed for the control system of the high-speed cruise missiles. The engineers of the Revolutionary Guard did not even recognize our defense mechanism and that's a good thing. We found a way to use a deepfake that simulates me as the source making the final destination where we strike. This will of course be known to only a few secret associates…"

"All right, Madani, you have reassured me. Please write a response for the supreme leader's eyes only," Kashani confirmed, "it also seems to me that at this stage we should inform the leader of the additional elements of the operation and above all specify our targets and the names of the important figures we recommend hitting."

***

Madani, who was closely monitoring the development of the Iranian version of the supersonic cruise missile, welcomed the daily assistance that the Russian engineers were giving to the project. He insisted that the airborne task force includes a sophisticated system for launching one cruise missile and keeping the other as backup. The timing for firing, Madani asserted, will only be when the MiG 31 planes arrive at the launch location. The determination of the location of the target will be with deepfake technology commands as ordered by Madani. All of this information was included in the document prepared at the request of General Kashani and delivered directly into the hands of the supreme leader.

Chapter 28

TEL AVIV

Dan Avni began preparing himself to lead the team of young people assigned to tackle the spy cell issue that the FBI reported on in the United States. The more he looked into it, the more slippery and unclear the subject seemed. He had eagerly accepted the request of senior advisors Gideon and Dieter to make a series of tests and studies, and he knew there were no better experts than Noam and Eric, and was sure they could solve the disturbing riddle. Dan also asked Evyatar to join the effort. The little information that could be helpful included the data that Deutsch passed on, and the results of research by Evyatar and his men that still did not manage to clarify what was actually happening with this Israeli espionage ring, if there was one at all...

"We are entering a different arena than the fight against terrorism, where we have a lot of experience and quite a few achievements," Dan began, "At the same time I am sure that the expertise we have each gained individually, and as a team, will help us collect the necessary data to analyze correctly to crack this thing..." Dan paused for a moment and took a deep breath before continuing. "I heard Nahari define the situation between us and the United States as a difficult one, both politically and diplomatically. At least at this stage, the directors of the CIA and the Israeli Mossad are working simultaneously but in coordination, trying to understand what is happening and clearing away any suspicions." Dan turned to Evyatar. "As a first step, I suggest you tell us what you and your people know so far about the Israeli spy cell that the FBI claims was discovered."

"We have more questions than answers. On the face of it, it seems to us that these are hackers equipped with a broad digital signature, but we have not found their exact whereabouts in the real world. From analyzing the few clues we have, we think they may be located in Silicon Valley, despite the fact that we did not detect any connection this group had with technological enterprises there."

"Noam? Eric? Can you shed any light on this business? Something we haven't yet considered? Maybe something to do with machine learning and facial recognition technologies?"

Noam responded. "If Evyatar is right about the group being based in Silicon Valley, we should concentrate our efforts there. We know the area well and have friends among the young people in the various start-up companies. This could definitely be a way that will lead us to solving the mystery."

"I completely agree with Noam's assessment," Eric

confirmed. "And if I may, Dan, I would like to clarify the role of machine learning that helped Noam develop facial recognition algorithms. The goal of machine learning is computerized treatment of data from the real world to tackle a specific problem when a computer program cannot be written for it. This is a recognition problem that a human expert is able to solve, but cannot write the protocols for it in an explicit way. Machine learning's aims are predicting or discovering facts about the real world. Speech recognition systems can also use machine learning. Another example is recommendations based on a relationship between a random group of users presented with an assortment of different data and items. All of this, combined with Noam's facial recognition technology, can lead to solving the mystery confronting us."

"Thank you, Noam, and Eric for your input. Hopefully, we have found a way forward," said Dan. "But before we conclude here, I think there is one more point that is also a challenge. I mean the possible role of Moscow in creating this noise about an Israeli spy cell in the heart of the United States. When you think about Russia's intensive use of social networks and its mission to create divisions in US society, we can assume that this may be another instrument in the Russian toolbox; this time to stir up the relationship between Israel and the United States. All this is information that will help us handle the issue. Of course, we still do not know what the American experts will find, but it is important for both sides to have a common understanding and consensus regarding how to find a solution."

***

"I hope you've made some progress analyzing the information on the spy cell affair so that we can contribute from our side to our American friends," Nahari greeted Dan, Evyatar, Noam, and Eric.

"We're not there yet," replied Dan, "but at least we have identified directions and a course of action that we hope will enable us to move forward..."

"And just how do you intend to do that? I heard from the head of the CIA about a combined effort that has already yielded results. He didn't elaborate, but I am certain he has something."

"Our findings so far point us to a center of activity in Silicon Valley. We think there is hacker activity there, perhaps by amateurs who have found a very sophisticated way to humble the source or basis of their activity..."

"So what's the next step?" insisted Nahari, "Should we leave the Americans to follow the thread or maybe join them in Silicon Valley?"

"I consulted with Deutsch, who is aware of everything going on at SRI and he advised me that we need to work together with Stanford University in Palo Alto. Deutsch said he would put all the SRI's expertise at the disposal of the Americans so we can eliminate a crisis. He recommended that the head of the Israeli Mossad and the head of the CIA should have a conversation and seal the agreement."

"Good!" exclaimed Nahari. "I have no problem speaking with the head of the CIA to concentrate our efforts in Silicon Valley. Moving our research teams to Palo Alto is also a feasible step. But doesn't the investment of so much effort to solve the mystery of the so-called spy cell interfere with our dealing with the threats from Iran, North Korea, and especially the activities of Moscow?"

"I think," Gideon intervened, "that according to what Dan said, and from what I understood from Deutsch on combining our capabilities with Americans in Silicon Valley, that the concentration of efforts at Stanford will help us handle what the Iranians are calling the 'Great Revenge' operation."

Gideon continued, recalling his joint work with Deutsch in thwarting terrorist elements in Palo Alto. "It is that precise geographical location – Silicon Valley – where we can best work on solving the mystery of the spy cell as well as ensure defense capability against the 'great operation' that threatens us both – Israel and the United States."

Chapter 29

TEHRAN

"We have conducted a series of tests on the prototype missile and they were a huge success!" Madani reported to General Kashani excitedly when he entered the commander's office.

"I am glad to hear that, Madani, and now? What is the next step? Can you guarantee that we have everything we require for the 'Great Revenge' operation?" questioned Kashani, who remained skeptical. "I want to see with my own eyes a successful experimental launch of the missile before we inform the supreme leader about the 'huge success.'"

"As you please, Commander. We have a perfect model of a test missile that is already assembled under the wing of the MiG-31 from which the missile will be launched," Madani promised. "I will report back to you as soon as possible and we will be waiting for you in the control room."

"The experiment had better be a huge success this time as well, Doctor Madani. My visit will be with the presence of some of our 'friends' from the Revolutionary Guard, and it has to go perfectly!"

***

The control room was full of representatives from all the security agencies. Kashani was mindful of shaking hands with the generals from the technological division of the Revolutionary Guard who were seated in the front row, close to the tracking screens. Madani ordered the test to begin. Immediately the MiG 31 was seen taking off with the new missile attached underneath the wing. Absolute silence in the control room. Only the whispered countdown of the experiment manager was heard. "Proper ejection," he called out as the high-speed missile was seen ejecting from the wing of the launching aircraft. "Speed of the missile augmenting as planned... five minutes to impact..." the test manager continued.

"The command to pinpoint the target has been given," the test commander whispered. The missile was seen changing course, veering sharply to the left. "One minute to impact!" exclaimed the commander and everyone held their breath.

A moment later a flaming ball of fire appeared on the screen, accompanied by enthusiastic applause in the control room. "Very impressive indeed!" General Kashani exclaimed happily. "Thank you Doctor Madani, many thanks to our engineer friends from Russia and a special thank you to our development team in the Quds Force. We have an imposing system of elite technological power and now also a suitable tool for the operation's missions in the future. I now have no doubt that our high-speed cruise missile is comparable to the Russian Kinzhal and our version definitely succeeded. Madani, please tell us exactly what you will report to the leader for his final approval."

"I thought I would show the leader a video of the last stage of the experiment, where you see the impact of the missile on a target in the ocean," Madani replied, "And then, I will propose using the high-speed missile to eliminate the head of the CIA and the head of the Israeli Mossad. I recommend requesting approval of these targets as the primary aim of our 'Great Revenge' attack. We have ongoing information from our hidden network in the United States that there is an upcoming meeting planned in Silicon Valley, California..."

"And how will we assure the leader that we know details about the enemies' meeting; when and precisely where it will take place?" Kashani posed the question.

"A crucial point, Commander. The answer is complex. Our agents are equipped with swarms of tiny drones that can camouflage themselves and avoid detection. In fact, they are already deployed and transmitting data from key areas in the valley. We have additional backup, Commander, which will ensure the successful execution of the mission..."

"What backup do you mean? Am I permitted to know as well?" Kashani allowed himself a rare smile.

"Of course, Commander," Madani reassured him, "you no doubt recall that we heard from the Russians about an organization called the 'Wagner Group.' This is an organization run by Yevgeny Viktorovich Prigozhin, an oligarch who is very close to President Putin. He is ready, following Putin's special approval, to serve us."

"I remember the name 'Wagner' but what is the connection to our issue?"

"These are Russian mercenaries, a kind of 'ghost army' of special forces. It is a quasi-private company accountable to the government in Moscow. It enables the Kremlin to operate secretly without being acknowledged directly by Russia. It is estimated that today between 6,000-8,000 personnel are working within the company. The Wagner Group operates in the field in full coordination with senior military commanders in target areas. If something happens that does not align with Russian interests and could embarrass the administration, the Kremlin will deny any connection to this force and its people who do Russia's dirty work. The Wagner group has in actuality become an arm of the Russian military. We know that Prigozhin responded to Putin's order and he will stand at the head of a group of fighters awaiting our requests."

"As far as I am concerned, everything you have just described can be presented at the meeting with the leader. I like the combination of the fast missiles along with backup from the ranks of the Wagner group. I have no doubt that this is convincing and guarantees that we will gain the approval and support of the supreme leader," declared General Kashani.

Madani continued. "There is one other thing, and it is highly classified. A two-step code will be embedded in the missile activation command. The missile will use both a sound file and a video file to lock onto the trajectory. I used my video image and voice for the encoding because I do not want anyone else to know about it. Without the coding, it will be impossible to guide the missile's trajectory or to deflect it."

"Excellent thinking. Another layer of defense always helps!" said General Kashani.

Chapter 30

TEL AVIV

"We struck gold on Iran's communications media!" Evyatar happily announced when Gideon and Dieter came to meet him in the surveillance room. "It's about the supersonic cruise missile the Russians are helping them build. Missiles similar to the Russian Kinzhal but made in Iran," he added.

"We've known about that project for a long time," commented Gideon, "What exactly is new about it? What's so important to make you say we struck gold?"

"Did they complete the project?" Dieter joined in and asked, "Do you know about any update the supreme leader received on the progress of its development? And what is happening with the Revolutionary Guard? We know that they weren't happy, to say the least, that the project was given to the Quds Force."

"The answers to both your questions are yes and yes," replied Evyatar confidently.

"We accessed the technological network of the Quds Force and recorded everything about the final stage of development for the cruise missile. We have a complete file of the final test and we can see clearly how the launch plane ejects the missile. It's a Russian MiG 31, of which Iran has several in their air force. We haven't yet deciphered the command sent to the plane prior to the release of the missile towards its target. A two-step code is embedded in the missile activation command. Both a sound file and a video file are used to lock onto the trajectory. We caught Madani saying he alone used coding in the video and his own voice, for security reasons. We've already forwarded the file of the experiment for Noam and Eric to review. Dan is also in the picture and will assist them in cracking the activation codes for the missile."

"You should also give Dieter a copy of the test you recorded," said Gideon, "He's studied the technological aspects of the Iranian version of the missile in greater depth than the rest of us. It is important to identify the countermeasure capability of the planes themselves already in the flight phase toward the target and before the release of the missile. And as for the attack order, I'm sure that Dan, Noam and Eric will find a way to neutralize the original command to the missile by replacing it with another."

"There's something else which Noam and Eric dealt with under Dan's guidance. I am talking about the spy cell that the FBI brought to our attention, and that's not resolved yet," Evyatar spoke up. "We have to find out what is really happening with regard to espionage and discuss it at the highest level. It's been agreed, if I'm not mistaken, that a meeting between the head of the CIA and the head of the Mossad would take place in Silicon Valley and there it will become clear to all of us of what's behind the FBI's claim."

"Right, Evyatar," said Dieter, "I can report that Dan, Noam, and Eric were able to home in on Silicon Valley and they raised the possibility of hackers there – amateurs, but with considerable skill and a love for Israel that's gotten a little out of control. If this turns out to be the case for the American side's inquiries as well, we can put this affair behind us."

"Let's assume that Noam and Eric are right, as we have just heard from Dieter," Mused Dan out loud, "and that the Americans will also come to the same conclusions when they look into this affair. We still have to concern ourselves about the meeting between the heads of our intelligence organizations and the threat that could do severe damage to us, both politically and from the security perspective," cautioned Dan. "Evyatar, we need to continue analyzing the information coming in about the Iranian threat and relaying our findings to the top personnel of the intelligence agencies – ours and the United States." continued Dan, "We know from past experience that systematic effort and in-depth analyses will enable us to devise a defense against the threat."

"We still don't know all that we need to about this." Gideon tried to summarize, "We have to get ready to deploy to the Silicon Valley area, especially near the SRI Institute. Dr. Deutsch has prepared everything necessary for the meeting between the Director of the CIA and the head of the Mossad to resolve the spy cell issue. But it is equally important for all of us to pre-

pare for the Iranian threat to hit the heads of our intelligence organizations. And Moscow's covert aid to Iran
requires our special attention."

"True, Gideon. The Iranian threat is being reinforced
by Russia," added Dan, "Information obtained by
Evyatar's media surveillance team revealed the intention to utilize the high-speed cruise missiles that Russia helped Iran develop. But equally disturbing is the
mobilization of the Wagner group to assassinate the
leaders of the CIA and the Mossad..."

"Yes, Dan, it's a double threat to the CIA and the
Mossad," Dieter also confirmed, "The 'Wagner Group'
is an operational arm of the Kremlin. The Russians'
use of clandestine forces to fight in arenas where they
have interests is not something new," Dieter continued.
"During Putin's rule as president, Russia has increased
these secretive conflicts. Five or six other such companies have been organized there and they all have ties
to Russian intelligence. The main one is the Wagner
Group, which has become an executive arm of the Russian military..." Dieter declared.

"If I'm not mistaken," Dan spoke up, "Russia activated the Wagner group on a large scale in Syria, assisting Assad against the rebels who tried to bring down
his regime."

"Absolutely, Dan!" Dieter rejoined, "I know that the
Wagner group, the Kremlin's ghost fighters, was operating in Syria for at least two years informally, until 2015,
when Russian involvement became official. Even today,
several hundreds and maybe thousands of mercenaries from the Wagner group are inside Syria. Apparently,

the deadliest event that the Wagner group was involved in was in February 2018. They participated in an attack in Syria together with Assad's army against pro-American organizations that included advisors from US Special Forces units."

"Important information for us, and equally important for the Americans," concluded Gideon,

"So...we're all agreed that the double threat to the CIA and Mossad has to be a top priority for the summit meeting between the two heads of intelligence..."

Chapter 31

MOSCOW

President Putin called an urgent meeting of the Politburo. The invited generals waited apprehensively in the briefing room for Putin to enter. Included were Defense Minister Sergei Korchenko, General Igor Kostkiukov, the head of military intelligence, and Air Force Commander Andrey Gomeny. Only the defense minister knew what Putin wanted to hear from them at the meeting.

All rose as one and saluted as the President entered, accompanied by his deputy.

"Greetings, gentlemen," Putin began calmly, unlike his usual demeanor. They knew that the president had something serious brewing. Absolute silence reigned in the room as the President gazed intently at one general after another, and they all wondered who would be sent to the gallows this time.

"I am worried, comrades. I have received a very unfavorable report directly from Dr. Madani, our Iranian contact. I would like to hear first from you, Defense Minister Korchenko, and then from the commander of the Air Force. Sergey, do you know about these difficulties Iran is having that Madani told us about?"

"I can happily report, Your Honor, that we were able to re-establish protection for the weapon convoys. They are being escorted – with the help of our anti-aircraft systems – on their way to Hezbollah in Lebanon. Two such convoys have already passed safely and are in Hezbollah's hands…"

"But what about the convoys through Syria, Sergey," scolded Putin, "I want to hear what we know about Iran's preparations for their 'Great Revenge' operation. And why are they having repeated disruptions of their media communications?"

"Ah…I will get to that right away, Your Honor. Indeed, the Iranians had some problems in preparing for their launch of the supersonic cruise missile. You approved giving them this technology and they are grateful, based on everything I have heard from my people. It should be mentioned that we still have a professional team in Tehran working with Iranian engineers on their version of the Kinzhal missile."

"If I may add, Honorable President," the Air Force commander spoke up, "the Iranians are basing their major operation on a MiG-31 aircraft to launch their cruise missile. The new development is the rapid ejection of the missile. We have heard, Comrade Putin, that there was a malfunction of the communication system that is supposed to direct the missile to the target. But we can hear more about that from our head of intelligence, General Kostkiukov."

"Igor?" Putin now quickly put pressure on Kostkiukov.

"What do we know about this malfunction in communication we have just heard the Air Force commander point out?"

"This is not something new, Your Honor," the head of intelligence hastened to answer, "We in Russia are also dealing with cyber-attacks and with threats that Artificial Intelligence and the algorithms derived from them, which makes them even more troublesome. Iran is obviously having more of a hard time dealing with such threats..."

"This is unsatisfactory," Putin continued the pressure, "What do we need to do so that the Iranians can move forward safely with their 'Great Revenge' operation?"

"Iran has a close relationship with North Korea, especially with its hacker center. I would recommend, sir, putting a team of our best scientists in the field of communications at Dr. Madani's disposal, as he is in charge of the Iranian revenge scheme. Our scientists will aid them until the execution of the operation."

"Enough with the talking," Putin snorted as he banged on the conference table, "I order immediate support be given to Iran for their operation! This will force the United States and Israel into a corner in the Middle East. Iran's intention is to hit the leaders of our two enemies' organizations, the CIA and the Mossad. They are deserving of our support, of course, without exposing our part in it. I understand that the combination of Artificial Intelligence, deepfake, and advanced cyber acts is a terrifying strategic threat to all parties. The technological team, which General Kostkiukov proposed, must be immediately deployed to assist Dr. Madani and ensure the proper functioning of the Iranian communications system for the missile. Also, you are to alert Yevgeny Prigozhin, in charge of the Wagner group strike force who are already positioned in Silicon Valley, to go into immediate standby mode!"

Chapter 32

STANFORD UNIVERSITY

Deutsch was careful to maintain the confidentiality of the meetings by scheduling them at various sites around the university. He continued coordinating between the two teams and introduced the members of the Israeli teams to the Americans. Ostensibly, the purpose of the meetings was to compare intelligence information the Israeli Mossad had on the one hand and the CIA, together with the FBI, on the other. Nahari accepted the proposal of the head of the CIA to combine the American and Israeli teams to uncover the truth about the alleged spy cell. The Americans agreed with the Mossad's assessment that the location of the cell would be somewhere in Silicon Valley. The American research team, at the same time as the Israelis, had already moved into buildings that Deutsch had arranged for them on the university campus.

"Good morning to you, my Israeli friends," Deutsch greeted the young people who had already been working hard for the past two days. "How are you settling in? Have you gathered any additional information from

Silicon Valley on the espionage cell? Are you ready to meet your American colleagues?"

"Good morning, it's good you came now," replied Evyatar. "We've had two crazy days. Our communication system crashed..."

"I wondered why I hadn't heard from you. I assumed you were busy making progress. What now, Evyatar? Have you got the communication system back up and running?"

"Yes, Deutsch, thanks to Dan, together with Noam and Eric, who went without sleep for two nights in a row and got our system working again. Do you have time to join the assessment review we're doing for Gideon and Dieter? We have some new information that came with the help of Noam and Eric from their Silicon Valley media searches, and Dan also pointed out that there was a threat coming at us from Russia..."

"Certainly, Evyatar, I'd be happy to join you and I would be honored to meet Gideon and Nimer here. I am glad to hear about your activity to thwart the Iranian-Russian threat. It won't come as a surprise to you that your American partners are also dealing with this issue. I recommend you both meet to coordinate data and situation assessments."

***

Evyatar's review went on for a long time, with Dan, Noam, and Eric occasionally adding their perspectives to the assessment. Gideon and Dieter, as well as Deutsch, listened with interest to the reports presented by Evyatar and his team. Gideon praised the young people and said that now that Iran's 'Great Revenge' operation is clearer, it allows for adequate preparation to prevent it. Gideon expressed hope that the spy cell case presented by the FBI would be cleared up by Noam and Eric, and by the experts of the American intelligence agencies, and would no longer be an issue. Dieter and Deutsch nodded their heads in support of Gideon. Additionally, Dan, Noam, and Eric informed them that they were working on a voice and video deepfake file that would be a key to the missile's two-step security code. They hoped it would trick the missile into sensing it was receiving contradictory commands and neutralize it.

Noam spoke up.

"With your permission, gentlemen from the United States, I will share with you what we learned from our research. Special thanks to you for the information which you have provided us. It was extremely helpful. Dr. Eric Grossfeld and I, after some challenging investigations, located the source of the spy cell coming from somewhere in Silicon Valley. Dan Avni, who was involved, supported this finding. We're glad to hear that you agree with it and are joining with us to try to pinpoint the source's precise location."

"Thank you, Dr. Noam Avni. Indeed, we accepted your conclusions about Silicon Valley being the source of the spy cell," responded the head of the FBI team. "It was very difficult to pick out the exact source from among the hundreds of start-ups in the Valley. Unfortunately, we have not yet reached a definite conclusion..."

"We had exactly the same problems to pinpoint the source," Eric agreed, "Fortunately, we found clues that helped Noam run the algorithms she developed for facial expression analysis technology and we now have a full analysis of the group that was the source of that spy cell...which actually did not really exist."

"What did you find out? What is the whole story?" The head of the FBI team asked excitedly, with the entire American team looking on with curiosity.

"The answer is a bit stupid and also maybe a little bit funny," replied Noam, "It was a group of young American Jews involved in ventures based on AI technology. They are amateur hackers who, either by luck or ingenuity, came up with a cyber defense that is very difficult to crack. These young people thought they were helping Israel in this way..."

"And you contacted them? What is the situation now?" The FBI man pressed.

"We didn't contact them because we thought this was your territory and we didn't want to intervene," said Noam.

"That was the proper thing to do," Deutsch said and then directed his remarks to the FBI team. "I suggest you take this thread to the end and conclude the affair. I will inform the head of the CIA and the head of the Mossad that they will hear the details from you about this bizarre 'spy cell' that did not actually exist and we can take it off the agenda."

For the next hour, a lengthy discussion took place between the Americans and the Israelis under the astute and sensitive direction of Deutsch. Only when all the information about the hackers who had played at being spies for Israel was revealed, did Deutsch decide that the issue was completely clear and it was possible to call the American and Israeli intelligence chiefs together to tell them about the resolving of this issue.

***

"Welcome to the 'holy of holies' of our institute," Deutsch greeted the heads of the intelligence organizations when they entered the laboratory, which was built ten meters underground. "This place has been determined by the Pentagon to be the safest both from the bombardment of warheads that can penetrate concrete, and in terms of electronic concealment," Deutsch emphasized proudly. "Soon you will hear a short summary from Dr. Noam Avni from Israel and then from the senior representative of the FBI.

Dr. Avni, the floor is all yours," said Deutsch.

"I am pleased to present to you, my dear sirs, our conclusions regarding the spy cell, which we reached by working together," Noam began with confidence. "We began to monitor messages emanating from Silicon Valley using AI tools and cyber algorithms. We found that deepfake technology helped to significantly reduce the number of companies that we needed to check out in depth. I suggest we hear from our American colleagues who had the same problem of narrowing the search to the most relevant companies."

"Noam is exactly right," confirmed the senior representative of the FBI, "We found hundreds of start-up companies in Silicon Valley of various sizes, and we could not manage to home in on just one. We very much appreciate the Israeli team finally identifying it, allowing us all to relax."

"The bottom line, gentlemen," Noam concluded, "is that we found the source. It's a little strange and a somewhat childish story of a group of young Jewish people, amateur but talented hackers, who thought they were helping Israel with their ruse..."

"The Israeli team gave us the details of the startup company and we will deal with them in an appropriate manner," added the FBI representative. Nahari and the CIA Director were relieved to hear the truth behind the so-called Israeli spy cell. They thanked the two teams that brought the issue to an end and thanked Deutsch for his assistance that led to a successful conclusion of the affair.

Chapter 33

TEHRAN AND STANFORD

Doctor Madani gathered his best men in the operation's surveillance room. All the walls in what Madani's team called "The War Room" were covered with huge display screens.

"What is the status of the two planes at the air force base near Tehran that are carrying the missiles?" Madani demanded of his aircrew chief. "I requested a further check to assure the readiness of the planes for the mission and to report to me the condition of the four missiles, two for each MiG 31."

"We have done so carefully, Commander," replied the air crew chief, "Everything was checked for the thousandth time, and the pilots, each with their navigator, are ready to take off the moment they receive the order from us. I remind you, sir, that one plane will take off and the other will wait as backup if, God forbid, the first one fails to launch the missiles."

Madani turned to the head of the Quds Force global communications team. "What do you know about the status of the force from the Wagner Group? Are we certain that they have not been exposed?"

"I checked with the Wagner group task force commander, Dr. Madani. He is absolutely sure that their presence has not been discovered. He is prepared to enter the secret burrow of the leaders of the CIA and the Israeli Mossad and eradicate them off the face of the earth."

***

"I believe, General Kashani, that we have covered all the elements for the Great Revenge operation," Madani said as he entered the general's office for a final update. "We have prepared sufficient backup arrangements for the mission to be accomplished no matter what."

"That is good, Madani, it appears you have covered all the operational tasks for the mission, but what about the communication systems? We remain here in Tehran and the planes with the missiles fly over the ocean. The Wagner group task force is on the other side of the world. In addition," Kashani continued, "we are using here for the first time Artificial Intelligence algorithms that we did not have before. Our dependence on deepfake technology is disconcerting."

Madani was silent for several moments and turned to adjusting something on the powerful computer he used constantly. Kashani looked intently at Madani and waited for answers.

Finally, Madani turned to him. "I would like to remind you, General, of the Russians' contribution to the security of our communication systems. They are in possession of the best protection software that exists in the world for everything related to Artificial Intelligence and its derivatives. The only detail we did not share with our Russian friends is the activation code for the missiles to guide their path to the target in the final stages of the flight. We practiced running the code only once in a full exercise so as not to reveal it to the enemy."

"Nice Madani. I am happy to hear that we are using Russian technology in the best possible manner."

***

Dr. Deutsch reserved an entire floor for the Israeli team in one of the university's buildings near the SRI Institute. The place was comfortable and safe and the Israelis effortlessly activated all surveillance and counter-measures against the Iranian threats. The American team, with representatives from the FBI and a technological group from the CIA, were also allotted an entire floor for all the listening and decoding equipment they needed. Gideon, who was in constant touch with the Americans, heard from them that a "Navy Seals" commando unit was in Silicon Valley monitoring the movements of the Wagner Group and was on standby to neutralize them.

"The first MiG 31 aircraft has received an order from Madani to take off," Evyatar called out, "They have thirty minutes of flight over the ocean until the launch of the high-speed missile."

"Two of our F-35s are taking off right now, to intercept it before it releases the high-speed missile," Gideon exclaimed, "I am informing the American team. Evyatar, did you activate surveillance for our planes on their way to intercept?"

"Yes! We're tracking them and you can see it on the screen here on the left," replied Evyatar, unable to contain his excitement. "There! The Iranian plane has been hit. You can see the left engine in flames. The pilots managed to eject but the aircraft is plunging into the water."

"Impressive coverage, Evyatar. Keep tracking, the next steps will come in a second. I am updating Nahari and the head of the CIA."

***

At the same time in Tehran...

"What is going on, Madani? Where is our plane? Are they all right and on schedule?" General Kashani demanded when he entered the war room.

"Aha! I see it now on the screen! Do you have communication with them?"

"Yes, Commander," Madani replied with a mixture of pride and concern. "The pilot reported what we saw, and has a few more minutes of flight until the release point for the missile..."

Absolute silence reigned in the war room as everyone in Madani's surveillance team was glued to their screen. Madani himself positioned himself in front of the camera with a direct connection to the MiG 31 and rehearsed for the umpteenth time the text he would use to lock the missile's trajectory on the final target to ensure a precise hit.

Suddenly a frenzied shout. "Enemy planes on either side of me!" The pilot of the MiG 31 was heard shouting.

"Enemy planes? What's going on??" cried Madani.

"Israeli F-35 aircraft and they are signaling me to turn west and not continue flying south..."

"Do not divert!" shouted Madani, "Go straight to your mission!" he commanded. In the next few seconds, the whole war room held its breath, hoping that everything would somehow work out...

"I've been hit! Left engine on fire!" The pilot's voice was now barely audible.

"Trying to eject..." the connection with the plane was lost. Madani knew he had to activate the backup plans immediately. There was no time to waste and he ordered the second MiG 31 to take off immediately but to fly at an extremely low altitude above the water in order to avoid enemy radar.

At the same time, Madani asked for contact with the Wagner group commander.

"Start moving toward your target. We activated the second plane because the first one was shot down by enemy planes. Are you up to date on information received from your tiny swarms?" Madani could not conceal his distress after the failure of the first plane shot down by the Israeli enemy. "How does access to our two targets in the SRI institute look to you?"

"We are on our way to the institute. We are mixed in among groups of ordinary students on campus. We checked a few days ago on how to gain entry to the institute and everything has been prepared to carry out the mission. Trust us, Your Honor, we have been in this scenario quite a few times before..."

***

"Another MiG 31 plane has taken off from the Iranian Air Force base," Evyatar called out. "It is flying at an extremely low altitude and is at risk of crashing into the ocean water. We think it's to avoid radar tracking. But wait! What's going on there?" Evyatar shouted, "There are two Russian Sukhoi Su-57 planes in the air flying at high altitudes... maybe this is the security that Moscow promised Iran?"

"Continue following the three planes," urged Dan, who kept his eyes peeled on the screen in front of him.

"The MiG 31 has another half hour until the release of the high-speed missile on its final leg to the target. That allows us leeway to continue tracking."

***

"What is going on, Madani? Are you still in control? Is it progressing as planned?" General Kashani kept asking extremely troublesome questions. He had not yet recovered his calm after the downing of the first MiG 31 before it had managed to launch the high-speed missile.

"Everything is under control, Commander," Madani tried to reassure him. "The second MiG 31 has taken off and is flying at my command at a very low altitude over the water to avoid enemy radar..."

"And that is all?" Kashani persisted, "And what guarantee is there that we won't fail with this one?"

"Commander, a contingency plan has been activated," Madani answered, as patiently as he could, "The Russians have sent two advanced fighter jets to escort our plane from high altitude. This should ensure that we do not have a repeat of the failure of the first plane. I have also been in contact with the commander of the Wagner task force and have given him instructions to start moving from his concealed location toward the SRI Institute. They are preparing to carry out the assassination of the director of the American intelligence organization and the Israeli."

"All right, Madani, all right." Kashani sighed in relief. "Just let it be successful this time!" Madani quickly typed in the two-step verification command and his voice and video file were activated. With the protection of the Russian escort planes, all that remained was for the deadly missile to hit its designated target...

Chapter 34

STANFORD AND TEHRAN

A tense silence prevailed in the control center of the Israeli team. No one uttered a sound. All eyes followed the Iranian MiG-31 on the screen. Noam and Eric sat side by side glued to their keyboards, waiting for activation of the countermeasures.

"Now everything is in your hands!" Dan called out to Noam and Eric, "Thirty seconds to launch!" Eric lowered his arm.

"Deepfake preparation command executed!" He called out from the keyboard. A muffled explosion was heard. Everyone held their breath as Noam confidently keyed in the activation of the deepfake. The high-speed missile could be seen detaching from the plane's wing and continuing south while gaining speed. The sound and video files simulating Madani's face and voice were activated at the same time, but the deepfake file that Noam and Eric had worked on was also activated. Now it just remains to be seen if the protocol would succeed in diverting the missile from its course.

"The missile is heading west!" Noam and Eric called

out simultaneously and a sigh of relief was heard throughout the room. "It received Madani's command and our deepfake order at the same time and dived right into the ocean!"

Shaking of hands, pats on the back for Noam and Eric, and applause echoed throughout the room.

"Dieter and I are going to the SRI Institute," Gideon announced, "We will let them know about this and see how to prepare for the remaining threats."

"I'm going to the Americans' control center to make sure they're tracking the developments." announced Dan.

"Dan, it's really happening!" said Noam. "Can you check if they received the information we gathered? I mean what we achieved with the help of the tiny drones and the facial expression recognition algorithms I passed on to them."

"Indeed, that's the most important thing right now," Eric interjected, "and if I am not mistaken, handling the remaining Iranian-Russian threat lies with the Americans, right?"

***

"The supreme leader is requesting a report on the failed launch of the high-speed missiles. I do not understand. What happened and how did it happen!?" General Kashani demanded as Madani entered.

"I am sorry, Commander, we did our best and lost the technological battle..."

"The leader has been informed of our fiasco, yours

in particular, from the Revolutionary Guard, of course." Kashani was outraged. "You must explain to me, Dr. Madani, before we go to the leader's office why exactly did we fail. The Quds Force, and especially you personally, are at a critical juncture. Your and our future is on the verge of removal..."

"I am deeply sorry, Commander, and acknowledge the failure of the airborne operations. They changed everything in the planning of the missile launch, which seemed completely successful in trials. We learned from the first failure, when our plane was shot down by the Zionist enemy, and we placed our trust in the Russians with fighter planes protecting our aircraft. Everything was functioning properly and the missile did indeed begin to fly after being launched..."

"And yet our new supersonic cruise missile, which passed all the tests, failed. Why did it not reach the target?"

"Commander, the missile was diverted from its course. Our technologists claim that it was due to interference of a deepfake technique that the enemy scientists developed. Unfortunately, they seem to be ahead of us in this area."

"Well, Madani, you will present all this to the leader in a few minutes. And you must also update us on the remaining mission for the great operation."

"Yes, commander, we have a ground operation already underway..."

"You mean the Wagner Group task force? That is what we have left?"

"Yes, General Kashani, this is Russia's additional

contribution to the revenge operation on the United States and Israel. Two minutes ago, I had secret contact with Yevgeny Prigozhin, who is in charge of the Wagner Group leading our task force. He informed us of a scouting patrol conducted two days ago, by fighters from his force, right inside the SRI Institute without being exposed. Yevgeny sounds confident in himself and in the ability of his men to complete the mission."

"Well," Kashani remained doubtful, "this must be explained to the supreme leader. Woe to us if we fail in this as well!"

Chapter 35

STANFORD

"Good that you joined me here at the institute." Deutsch greeted Gideon and Dieter when they entered his office, "The Seals are here, taking strategic positions to stop the operation."

"We don't see them." commented Gideon, "There are only students around."

"Don't worry, my friend, the Seals only appear to be students..."

"The Wagner force may also be posing as students!" Dieter warned. "Has the face recognition data that Noam and Eric passed on to the American team been given to the Seals?"

"Yes, Dieter, everything was passed on to the commander of the Seals who are currently manning the entrance to the only elevator that allows entry to the protected underground area.

"Come with me and see it with your own eyes..."

Deutsch led Gideon and Dieter to the elevator when a group of students overtook them and advanced rapidly into the corridor.

"The Wagner Group!" Dieter exclaimed, "We have to stop them!"

Just then another group of "students" rushed past Deutsch and the crack of automatic gunfire echoed loudly throughout the corridors.

"I'm hit! My arm!" Deutsch moaned and Gideon and Dieter immediately went to him. "I'm okay, I'm okay," whispered Deutsch. "More important they take care of the Wagner force," he gasped to Deutsch while Gideon bandaged his wound to stop the bleeding.

"You are surrounded! Throw down your weapons and raise your hands!" shouted the Seal commander. Four fighters from the Wagner group lay wounded on the floor. Only their leader remained standing with his hands in the air. Two Seals quickly approached him and cuffed him without meeting any resistance.

***

The head of the CIA and the head of the Mossad gathered both teams, American and Israeli, in the institute's large conference hall. The commander of the Navy Seals and his deputy were there, along with Dr. Deutsch, who entered the hall with their support, his arm bandaged and in a sling. Resounding applause greeted their entrance.

"I am honored to say a few words about the successful prevention of a major Iranian operation with the aid of Russia," began the head of the CIA. "Thank you Mr. Nahari, head of the Israeli Mossad, and to all your people who have so impressed us with their proficiency and tenacity to achieve the best outcome. We thank them for their exceptional cooperation. Our gratitude must be extended also to our people from the CIA and the FBI, who made a considerable contribution to the success of the Iranian-Russian countermeasures. And a very special thanks to Dr. Deutsch, director of the SRI Institute, with whom we all worked to prevent this ominous threat from being realized. Thank you, Dr. Deutsch and a speedy recovery." The applause and cheers for Deutsch lasted a long time.

"With your permission, my friend, the head of the CIA, I would also like to add a few words of appreciation and gratitude," Nahari said. "Congratulations to the two teams, the American and the Israeli, who worked so well together and brought about the successful termination of a complex threat using a combination of advanced technology along with traditional anti-terrorist methods. Let me sum up...Due to this impressive cooperation, gentlemen, we eliminated the suspicion that an Israeli spy cell had been supposedly established and operating here in the United States. We then dealt with the major threat that Iran was preparing with Russian assistance, a matter of enormous concern. The threat was thwarted and the two teams, which coordinated superbly, deserve all our blessings."

Nahari paused and waited for the applause to end. "And last but not least, we wish to thank Dr. Deutsch for arranging for all of us to work together with confidence and mutual trust to overcome the threat from Iran and Russia. We will all do our utmost to make sure that in the future, Moscow will no longer be threatening us. And this, gentlemen, is thanks to you all." concluded Nahari and warmly shook hands with the head of the CIA.

"At your service, sirs," exclaimed the senior representative of the FBI, "a greeting has just arrived from our president with congratulations for such an important accomplishment. The president has ordered both teams to be decorated for extraordinary achievement in the defense and security of the United States and the State of Israel."

Printed in Great Britain
by Amazon

29854195R00138